His Royal Highness,
J. Aubrey Whitford

Also by Frank Roderus

His Royal Highness, J. Aubrey Whitford

FRANK RODERUS

A DOUBLE D WESTERN

DOUBLEDAY

New York   London   Toronto   Sydney   Auckland

A Double D Western

PUBLISHED BY DOUBLEDAY

a division of Bantam Doubleday Dell Publishing Group, Inc.
666 Fifth Avenue, New York, New York 10103

Double D Western, Doubleday,
and the portrayal of the letters DD
are trademarks of Doubleday, a divsion of
Bantam Doubleday Dell Publishing Group, Inc.

Library of Congress Cataloging-in-Publication Data

Roderus, Frank.
His Royal Highness, J. Aubrey Whitford/Frank Roderus.—1st ed.
    p.   cm.—(A Double D western)
I. Title.
PS3568.O346H57   1992
813'.54—dc20   91-44396
CIP

ISBN 0-385-26691-X

His Royal Highness,
J. Aubrey Whitford

ONE

ESMERALDAVILLE, Texas. The name was about two sylla-
bles bigger than the town. A poor stage for a player of substance. Still and all, if Esmeraldaville was all one had, why
then, Esmeraldaville was the clay one would mold to meet
one's need.

J. Aubrey Whitford firmed his jaw and adopted his best
and most dignified mien.

He was, he acknowledged, at considerably less than his
best.

Very much the fault of the miserable beast, um? Horseback. Such a *crude* form of transportation.

But then this *was* Texas. What could one expect? Even in
this modern era, this Year of Our Lord 18 and 52, Texas and
Texans had managed to mire themselves in the past. No
railroads. An uncertain post. No scheduled coach service to
speak of. Why, these people built their houses of *mud,* for
heaven's sake. It was all quite drearily uncivilized.

Yet it was what one was required to work with.

J. Aubrey sniffed loudly, almost lost his balance for a moment there and had to grab for the vertically emplaced knob
thing that was conveniently mounted on the front of his
saddle. Damn, but he did despise horses. Perching atop
them, that is. It was acceptable to ride in a properly sprung
vehicle behind them.

But to try to balance oneself on a horse's narrow, bounc-
ing back? That was more than uncomfortable. It was dangerous. One could fall. And it was a *long* way down.

J. Aubrey Whitford might make many claims—some of

them actually valid—but equestrian eptitude was a boast he would never proclaim. "Walk, horse, waaa-llllk."

He bounced, jigged and wriggled, struggling all the while to maintain a position more or less in the middle of the vile beast. His point at the moment was to avoid the fall he dreaded.

Still and all. . . .

A man does what a man must do. Homespun hooey to be sure, but in this case true.

J. Aubrey Whitford was, after all, a man on a mission. If that meant he had to ride a horse, then a horse he would ride.

He squared his shoulders. Lifted his chin. Hoped his collar had not begun yet to wilt. He would have reached up to finger it and make sure but that would have involved letting go of his grip on the saddle knob thing.

He wanted to present himself at his best to the townspeople of Esmeraldaville, Texas.

And please, please, please he would not fall off the damned horse while doing so.

"I'm coming, Grace. I'm coming," he muttered softly to reinforce his resolve.

TWO

A MAN, tall and thin and middle-aged, appeared in the open doorway of a storefront—one of the half-dozen or so that comprised what little there was of Esmeraldaville, Texas—and saw the rider's approach. The man stood there a moment and then withdrew. A moment later he was back and so were several others who stood in the doorframe gaping at the approach of a stranger.

Rustics, J. Aubrey thought happily. Gullible as sheep and twice as stupid. How convenient. A smile beamed down upon the natives like sharply focused rays from the Point Narrows light.

"Gentlemen. How *do* you do!" He dragged the horse to a nervous halt and slid gratefully down to terra firma. His knees shook and trembled; his backside ached; his eyes burned, and his head ached. My, but he felt good now that he was once again standing on his own two feet.

The natives were as unblinking as lizards. But alive. J. Aubrey could tell because one of them turned his whiskered head and spat a stream of dark juice into the sun-baked earth that served here as street, gutter and sidewalk alike. J. Aubrey's smile continued to lave them.

"Permit me, gentlemen, to introduce myself. I am, sirs, the honorable J. Aubrey Whitford. Esquire. Late of New York City."

He swept his hat off, that utilitarian gesture flowing into a grand sweep and a bow as he made a half-leg before them.

His impression, he was confident, was . . . not to be immodest about it, but nonetheless . . . the impression was dazzling.

Oh, he knew well enough what these Texas rubes could see. A gentleman, no less, and a grand gentleman at that. Tall at a mere hairsbreadth less than six feet. Broad of shoulder, stout of limb and narrow of waist. Dressed even in these primitive conditions in yellow waistcoat, crisp collar and silken cravat, wearing a dark gray swallowtail suit and a pale dove's belly gray top hat.

More important than the sartorial accoutrements, though, was the man himself, a distinction that J. Aubrey well understood. And he was, if he did so admit, well blessed in that regard.

His head was large even for his exemplary frame. His jaw was square and handsomely molded, and at the point of his chin there was a cleft placed as if by deliberate design where it lent an aura of rugged masculinity. His leonine mane of brown hair was thick and rich and full, extending far down his cheeks in the muttonchop style. His eyes were gold-flecked hazel, large and clear and encouraging of trust and confidence.

Men tended to view J. Aubrey Whitford with admiration. Ladies tended to view him with interest. He discouraged neither viewpoint.

Now he raised up from his small bow, smiled again . . . and recoiled back away from the advance of three—no, four, and there were others showing themselves behind this first bunch now too—suddenly scowling townsfolk. Scowling? They were positively furious. Inexplicably yet undeniably furious. And no small number of them as they began now to press into the doorway.

"G-gentlemen?" he sputtered.

"Whitford, y' say? J. *Aubrey* Whitford?" The local made the name sound an epithet. And a most disagreeable one at that.

"I have that honor, yes," J. Aubrey returned, his voice stout and sure. Inwardly, though, his bowel churned and turned watery, and he wondered if there was time enough to return to the saddle and seek an escape from these fools.

No time, he realized. Not, at least, for a gentleman who required a certain amount of assistance whenever he wished to mount the steed in question.

The smile came back in full force. J. Aubrey motioned airily toward his horse. "If one of you chaps would be good enough to see to my mount, gentlemen, we can continue this indoors, um? Perform the introductions over a dram, shall we? My treat, of course. Now stand aside there. That's right. Open the way for me. Step aside, you. Thank you."

He marched blithely to them. Through them. The irate townspeople of Esmeraldaville parted before him like the waves separating for Moses, and J. Aubrey Whitford sailed boldly into the lion's den.

THREE

J. AUBREY planted himself squarely in the center of things. But with his back placed judiciously to the store counter so that no one could insinuate themselves behind him without considerable bother. He propped one elbow on the countertop and with his other hand waggled the men of Esmeraldaville nearer. "Join me, um? Sarsaparilla for everyone, proprietor. Whichever of you fits that category, eh?" He smiled. And hoped he wasn't sweating so badly that it yet showed. A good many of the men in the crowd looked like they intended to do him bodily hurt.

Before him the townsmen appeared at least for the moment to be confused. Then again, their confusion was the whole idea of the bluff.

"Now, sirs," J. Aubrey said as if he hadn't a care in the world, "did I mistake your meaning just then or has my name reached your fair city ahead of me?"

"Say what, mister?"

"When I announced my name, gentlemen, there were several among you who gave the appearance of having heard it in advance of this moment. You, sir. I believe you are the fellow who responded. And in answer to your question, yes. I am indeed J. *Aubrey* Whitford. As, I believe, I stated already." He smiled. It wasn't easy, but he managed. He tried to present an appearance of unconcern. He wasn't so sure about that but believed he pulled it off fairly well under the circumstances. A smile is easily feigned. It requires only a certain manipulation of the lip, the display of a flash of teeth. Hardly a difficult exercise. The rest of the deception, however, needed an entire body posture to achieve the desired impression. And limp is not so easy to accomplish when one's flesh is crawling with apprehension.

"You son of a bitch," someone snarled.

The smile remained in place. "Is everyone here so rude? Or are you the town embarrassment?" he inquired cheerfully.

"I say we tar an' feather the SOB," another voice put in.

J. Aubrey clucked softly, as if to himself, and very sadly. "Rude indeed," he muttered just loudly enough for the men to overhear. "And so foolish."

"What's that?"

"Rude, I said," he repeated a little louder. "And foolish."

"We ain't the ones who—"

"You are the ones who are being rude and foolish," J. Aubrey persisted.

"How you figure—"

"Quite simple, gentlemen," J. Aubrey said in a well-oiled tone. "I make an appearance in this city for the first time. We can, I believe, agree upon that, um? I have not ever trod these streets before." An exaggeration, of course. There was but one street to tread. And that more by implication than design. The so-called street was merely a patch of barren earth where nothing happened to be growing at the moment. "Yet you become quite thoroughly unreasonable when I do no more than announce my name. Why, I daresay several of you ruffians act as if you would wish to cause me bodily hurt. Now I ask you this, gentlemen. What has been my reaction to all of this? Um? Have I attempted to flee? No? I suggest you ask yourselves why, instead of dashing away from your clutches, why have I walked in amongst you and requested refreshment? Which I remind has not yet been delivered. Proprietor, whichever you are, please correct the oversight. At once, my good man, at once. A sarsaparilla. And for whoever else cares for one."

"Listen, you—"

"No, you listen for a moment. You are angry. I presume

you have cause. But you are not angry with me. For this there is no cause. There cannot be. I have done harm to no man in this community. Nor to any woman. I have never been here before this very point in time. So what possible hostility could you hold for me? Can any man among you at least explain that much? Hmm?"

J. Aubrey sniffed and looked down as if to examine his fingernails. Now if only these imbeciles would refrain from pummeling him long enough for rational thought to take hold. . . .

"You don't look like no Janine Aubrey Whitford," one of the men said in an accusing tone.

"No, sir," J. Aubrey agreed. "Nor do you look like you should be called Barbara. May I ask what that has to do with anything?"

"Aubrey ain't your mother's maiden name?"

"I beg your pardon?"

"Your mama. Was Aubrey her maiden name?"

"Not that it is any of your business. But, no. It was not."

"Dammit, Harry, that part o' it was lies too. Every word that damn woman said was lies. All lies."

"Woman?" J. Aubrey exclaimed. "It was a woman who presented herself here under the name Whitford? Good Lord, man, tell me it's true."

"You know her?" someone asked.

"Yes, yes, of course I know her. She is the reason I've come here, you see. Now tell me, man. Where is she? What has she done to make you all so angry? Tell me everything, man, and quickly."

This time there was no need for him to falsify his expression, his posture, his sudden animation.

J. Aubrey Whitford's excitement this time was entirely genuine.

"Tell me, man, please, and I shall be forever in your debt."

"Interestin' you should bring up the word 'debt' there. Y'know?"

"Tell me. Please," he begged.

"You ain't gonna like this," the man named Harry warned.

"I daresay I shall like it better than being tarred and feathered."

"Yeah, you got a point there. Sorry 'bout that."

"Never mind all of that, man. Tell me about the lady who borrowed my name. Please, man. I must know."

"She ain't no good, Mr. Whitford. If that's who you really are, that is."

"Just tell me. You must."

The man shrugged and reached into his pocket for a plug of tobacco. Behind him the other men of Esmeraldaville looked like their anger was abating. A squat, powerfully built man broke out of the crowd and came behind the counter. He began setting out tin mugs and filling them with a sticky-sweet sarsaparilla root beverage. J. Aubrey considered it a significant improvement to discover that he himself was given the first mug.

Harry, who had agreed to tell the story, deliberately waited until the commotion died down and his listeners were silent around him. It was apparent that the tale would be new only to the visitor but that this was to be the sort of story that the townsmen would want to hear retold anyway, if only so they could remain current with its embellishments.

"The way it happened was this . . . ," Harry began.

FOUR

HE WAS ONLY a day behind her. Slightly less, actually. The news was enough to quicken J. Aubrey's heartbeat. It was, after all, the first real word he had had of her since she ran off from the wagon train those days past. Oh, Grace. Lovely Grace. Captor of his heart, possessor of his hope. Miss Grace. Perfect Grace. So perfect neither he nor she had known it at the time. He sighed. And paid attention to the last details of sad Harry's little tale.

J. Aubrey managed to maintain a dour expression throughout, sympathy oozing from his pores and drooling off his chin for all to see.

Inwardly he was laughing, chuckling, cheering Grace's efforts.

Oh, the girl had much to learn. But her instincts were sound. She had all the ingredients: the nerve and the wit and the will. It was only experience that she lacked. And that he would help her gain when once more he found her, held her in his arms, felt the warmth of her against . . . never mind *that,* ahem. He cleared his throat and concentrated on listening to the unhappiness of the rustic residents of Esmeraldaville, Texas.

J. Aubrey clucked and nodded and agreed with whatever they said. It was awful. Horrid. Perfectly unconscionable the way one could no longer place one's faith in one's fellow beings. J. Aubrey Whitford was a veritable study in sympathetic understanding.

And of course from their point of view the story was a sad one indeed.

A lady—whoever would have thought she was otherwise

—presented herself to them. A traveler, she said she was. Janine Whitford, she said she was. The victim of a brigand, she said she was. Robbed of all her possessions, she said she was. On a mission of the heart, she said she was. Unwilling to turn back no matter the trials that might lie ahead, she said she was. Ah, her honeyed words had torn at their hearts. As good men are wont to do, they offered to help.

Marks, bless them, J. Aubrey thought. They present themselves with such convenient regularity. Again he had to hide an inclination to smile.

The story in a nutshell was this: The pretty lady traveler had been robbed, but unbeknownst to the highwaymen she carried concealed within her cloak a number of bank drafts, each worth a thousand dollars upon signature and presentation. All her cash had been stolen but not these. They were made out to her as J.—standing, of course, for Janine—Aubrey—her mother's maiden name and hence by way of the custom her own middle name as well—Whitford.

Yes, the men of Esmeraldaville certainly understood such things. And when they heard the reason why this young and lovely lady was traveling alone, when they realized her need for a swift pursuit of her goal, why of course they volunteered their assistance without delay.

The makeshift tale only confirmed J. Aubrey's conviction that the girl had talent lying latent and strong, waiting only for his own learned guidance to bring it to full flower.

What she told them—there was not a shred of truth in it, to his own certain knowledge—was that her fiancé was in mortal danger somewhere on the road ahead. She had to find him, warn him, unite herself to him so they could live out their lives together. Otherwise, unknowing of his peril, the handsome lad—poor Harry said she'd wept at this point —would fall prey to the villains from whom she proposed to save him. The love of her life would be dead, and her own heart would perish with him. Two lives would be snuffed out in a single act of violence. And now—sob, sob

—she was out of funds and unable to replenish the stock of supplies that had been stolen from her.

The men of Esmeraldaville—they were honest men; they told their own failings as forthrightly as they told the rest— were the ones to suggest that they cash one of the drafts she carried. She would be able to resupply and have ample funds left over. And did she require a guide to help her find her way? Anything they could do, they would do.

The lady had agreed—not surprisingly—to cash a draft and purchase supplies. She declined the offer of a companion or companions to assist her on the road. She was frightened of strangers, she said, because it was in just such a way that she had fallen into the clutches of those who robbed her; she had thought they were offering to help when instead their only desire was to harm her. Or so she'd said.

Ah, it was all quite soul-wrenching, no doubt. The girl had given a sterling performance. J. Aubrey only wished he'd been present to observe and to applaud it.

And what, he now asked, made the upstanding and good-hearted gentlemen of Esmeraldaville comprehend their error?

Harry became grumpy at that point. A respected member of the community returned only last night—shortly after the lady rode away—from a visit to distant Fredericksburg. The vile and scheming woman—Harry's opinion, not J. Aubrey's —would have remained undetected at least until the bank draft failed to clear save for that arrival of the gentleman who'd been to Fredericksburg. Yes, that man swore, there was a Whitford who'd been traveling, and quite well heeled, with a group of gold seekers bound for the Baja. But Whitford was a man, not a lady. And there had been some difficulty at the bank in Fredericksburg, something to do with bank drafts? The fellow hadn't been sure of all that part. But he did swear that Whitford was as male as he himself because he himself had seen the expedition leader on the streets of Fredericksburg on at least two separate occasions.

In the company, he thought, of a most attractive lady. Who, yes, did fit the description of this woman who now passed herself as being Whitford.

It was at that point that the men of Esmeraldaville knew they'd been gulled. They had accepted a draft as genuine and paid out change for it, and now they had been stung to the tune of a full thousand dollars in cash and in kind, for part of the spurious earnings had been collected by the lady in the form of traveling supplies up to and including a horse to pack everything upon.

Oh, the people of the town had been duped and ill-treated, and they did not like it.

And when they thought that there was another among them who was part and parcel of this dishonesty, why, how else might a man react except with anger?

And come to think of it, dammit, what *was* Mr. Whitford's role in all this?

At which point dismay once again converted itself to anger, and J. Aubrey could feel the returning hostility of the men who crowded so close around him here.

"Never fear, gents," J. Aubrey said grandly. "I shall set this matter aright for you." He smiled. Leaned calmly against the countertop. Took a birdlike sip of the overly sweet sarsaparilla.

"How you gonna do that, mister?" someone demanded.

J. Aubrey smiled. And yawned. Give him just a second to think it up, he knew, and he would have an answer to that question. Although the full truth was that he would be interested to hear it himself. At the moment he hadn't yet a clue.

"To your good health, gentlemen," he said as he lifted his mug in their direction and bought himself more thinking time by that innocent delaying tactic.

FIVE

"THE LADY'S NAME is Grace," J. Aubrey said with a smile. It wasn't, actually. But it was the name she had given him, the name he himself knew her by, loved her by. It was quite unimportant what her name might truly be. And any designation would suffice for the purposes of the moment.

All around him eyebrows lifted as the men of Esmeraldaville recognized the gentleman's admission that he was acquainted with the lady who had so badly gulled them.

J. Aubrey merely continued to smile.

"You know her," someone growled, his tone of voice making it more accusation than statement.

"Of course I know her. Gads, gents. The girl's my sister, don't you see." The words came smooth and easy, never mind that J. Aubrey's intentions toward Grace were anything but brotherly.

"Your sister?"

"Indeed. Grace Elaine Whitford if you must know the whole of it. She only pretended otherwise because it was my name on the bank drafts. The drafts, you see, were actually mine. She, um, borrowed them. So to speak."

"Then them bank drafts—"

"Are perfectly genuine," J. Aubrey assured them. Inaccurately. But then they needn't know that. In fact had best not discover it. He smiled again. Took a sip of his depressingly sweet beverage.

"But they—"

"Come, come, gentlemen. Let's not burrow too deeply, shall we? No need for things to become unpleasant here, mm? Suffice it to say, the lady is my sister. The drafts, although genuine, were not hers to endorse. Her urgency, however, was as true as she claimed it to be. The fine young man who soon should become my brother-in-law is in peril, gentlemen. I cannot possibly begrudge Grace her efforts to save him. I understand and forgive her, um, momentary indiscretion."

"You mought forgive an' forget, mister, but we—"

J. Aubrey cut the man short with a wave of his hand. "I ask you to forgive and forget, gentlemen. But only after your losses have been made good. I would not expect you to be so sympathetic otherwise."

"You'd make good on what she went an' done t' us?" a worried Esmeraldavillian mumbled.

"I could do no less and still consider myself a gentleman, gentlemen. Naturally I shall indemnify you against loss."

J. Aubrey's was no longer the sole smile extant in the crowded store. All about him now there was a relaxation of the tensions that had been so high. The men of the ugly little settlement commenced to grin and scratch.

Ah, J. Aubrey thought, sheep are so very easily soothed.

SIX

J. AUBREY WHITFORD yawned and sipped at his sarsaparilla. He had things nicely under control now. He could feel it throughout this crowded room. The locals believed him, accepted him. A man could ask for no more than that.

Smoothly, making it up as he went along, he embellished the story Grace had sold them about this alleged fiancé of hers. Not that there was really any need for embellishment here. It was simply that as an artist, a true artist, J. Aubrey was enjoying the experience of creating the woof and weft to Grace's warp. He was, in fact, having fun now.

"You said somethin' about making good what we lost, mister?" a townsman finally reminded him.

"Indeed, sir. Indeed I did and indeed I shall." J. Aubrey smiled and set his now empty mug onto the general store counter. "I assume one of you has possession of my bank draft?"

"I do," the storekeeper said. He took a cigar box from beneath the counter, opened it and extracted an entirely familiar-looking document which he then handed over.

"Ah, yes." The document purported to be a draft against the First Continental Bank in far distant New York City. The document was in truth a magnificent forgery. J. Aubrey knew that for a fact because it was his own fine hand that had created it. He smiled again now.

"You can see whereat she signed it with your name, mister," the man called Harry said. He leaned closer and pointed.

The forged signature endorsing an already forged draft was amateurish but showed talent. With no more than a modicum of guidance—J. Aubrey would be only too happy to provide that education for the lovely girl—Miss Grace might well be able to blossom forth as a paper hanger in her own right. But first he had to find her, speak with her—she would be apprehensive, was bound to be, would almost certainly believe that he wanted to prosecute her even though nothing could be further from the truth than that— convince her of how pleased he was that she had stolen the bank drafts from him and thus had proven their compatibility as a twosome. Dammit! If only he could reach her.

"Yes," he said for the benefit of his unsuspecting listeners, "my dear sister's hand is very much like my own. But then we learned our letters from the same tutor, mm? No wonder you were taken in." He folded the document to its original creases and slipped it back inside his coat pocket where it belonged. The selfsame coat pocket from which Miss Grace had so recently extracted this draft and the others like it.

"What are you gonna . . . ?"

J. Aubrey smiled, dismissed the sudden concern with a wave of his hand. "The draft is good, of course. I could add a genuine signature to it, and it would be honored. But it would have to travel all the way back to New York before it would clear. I see no reason why you gentlemen should have to wait that long for your money."

The men of Esmeraldaville began to smile too now.

"Why don't I just replace the draft with something more readily negotiable, mm?"

"Cash, mister?"

"If I could, certainly. But I rushed away in pursuit of my dear sister quite as quickly as Grace rushed off in pursuit of my soon to be brother-in-law."

A few of the newfound smiles turned back to being frowns again.

"No need for you to be discommoded, gentlemen. While I haven't sufficient cash in my pockets at the moment"—in point of fact Grace had left him with, uh, *no* cash in his possession just now—"I have more than ample funds on deposit with the bank in Fredericksburg. Where your informant quite accurately represents me as having recently been." His smile never wavered. "Hand me a counter check if you will, sir," he said to the general store proprietor.

"You don't got any o' your own?"

"My sister in her haste seems to have, um, taken those with her too." He said it cheerfully enough. But with a hint of underlying sadness. Just that meager hint, a tightening at the corners of the eyes, a barely discernible faltering of the voice. J. Aubrey counted on the good people of Esmeraldaville to interpret this as brotherly love preventing him from openly accusing his sibling of the truth, which was that his own dear sister had stolen from him. Or so he wished these men to believe.

"I got some I expect you could use. You say it's t' be drawed on them Germans in Fredericksburg?"

"I did, sir. A fine bank, that. Entirely stable, I am told. Never any hints of scandal there."

"Can't argue with that, Mr. Whitford."

J. Aubrey smiled. Mister was *such* a pleasant title as compared with, say, SOB. Which was how he'd started out in this village.

"I shall write you out a check to replace the draft then, gentlemen. It shan't take so long to clear." He accepted a blank check, steel pen, bottle of prepared ink. Dipped nib in ink and bent over the bit of paper, where he paused. "By the way, gentlemen, I shall need supplies, a pack animal, very much the same sort of equippage my dear sister purchased for her journey. How much over the draft amount should I make this check so as to cover my, um, purchases as well?"

After all, a scam already proven is a scam tried and true. If Miss Grace could employ it on these innocents, why not J. Aubrey too?

SEVEN

AH, THIS WAS BETTER. Immeasurably so. J. Aubrey sat atop his horse—there had been no mounting block handy but a helpful townsman had consented to hold the beast's head whilst he reluctantly returned to the saddle—and turned to survey the dramatic improvements in his situation.

Now a burro trailed docilely at the end of a leash arrangement—lead rope the locals termed it—with a pack of supplies strapped to its back. The pack held J. Aubrey's Esmeraldaville purchases; foodstuffs, skillet, enameled steel coffeepot, assorted ropes and pegs and things. J. Aubrey quite frankly had no idea what most of those were or what their purposes should have been, but the men who were assisting him in his selection of camp gear included the items and he did not demur.

Most critically important so far as J. Aubrey himself was concerned, he had "bought"—a useful term even if not fully descriptive; there were, after all, no funds in the Fredericksburg bank to cover the check he'd passed here—a small quantity of paper and ink powders. The paper sheets were of the best grades locally available, a few sheets of each including silk and linen bond. With those a gentleman of J. Aubrey Whitford's talents could manufacture whatever financial instruments and personal documentation anyone might ever require. And in whatever names he might deem suitable, just in the happenstance that Miss Grace should have made the name Whitford unacceptable in these parts.

At the moment, though, J. Aubrey was quite thoroughly pleased with himself, with Grace, with all of life in general.

And of course with the good folk of Esmeraldaville in particular.

He balanced precariously atop his horse and beamed a benediction down upon the townsmen.

"Thank you. Thank you all for helping me."

"Thank *you* fer helpin' us," the spokesman for the group responded.

J. Aubrey smiled. It would take, he calculated, a minimum of six days, perhaps longer, before these sheep discovered that they'd been twice fleeced.

"The pleasure was all mine," he told them. Which was perhaps the most completely truthful thing he said to them. "Good day, gentlemen." He rapped his heels against the sides of the horse and bobbed off in the direction they said Grace had traveled before him.

EIGHT

J. AUBREY GROANED. Shifted position. Winced aloud as once more the nagging pains stabbed through his flesh. He was sore as a boil from sitting in that saddle. In fact he would not be surprised to discover that he was developing boils. Probably it was just as well that he couldn't see to examine the particular spot in question. He groaned again and reached for the pot of water he'd set on the fire.

Coffee, he thought, would improve his disposition and help to settle the queasiness that churned in his stomach at the moment. Salt pork charred on the outside and rubbery raw within had done nothing to satisfy his appetite.

He found the cup he'd bought back in Esmeraldaville and tipped the pot over it. Water with a pale tint of yellow spilled out into the cup. It neither looked nor smelled much like coffee even though it had been heating at a boil for twenty minutes or longer. Surely that should have been long enough to make coffee. Yet it hadn't. J. Aubrey frowned. He'd never made claims about being a cook. Just as well too. That was a deception even his extreme powers of persuasion would be incapable of supporting.

He sniffed, scowled and took a sip of the brew he'd created. It tasted no more like coffee than it smelled the role. But at least it was hot. He drank some more of it.

While he did so he peered off into the night. Having just been looking into the fire he could see nothing despite the starlight and the presence of a newly risen moon. Not that there was anything out there to see anyway.

J. Aubrey shivered.

There was no other human . . . no other habitation . . .

no voice nor smile nor mark of man . . . nothing that he knew of for uncounted miles in any direction.

He was alone. The experience proved to be unnerving. Unique, at least in his own past experience. He didn't *like* it.

Here, with nothing but a horse and a burro for companionship, J. Aubrey Whitford had only his own resources to lean upon. And his fields of expertise did not happen to include solitary travel in the wilderness. He shivered again and tried to warm himself with another swallow of the non-coffee.

If only . . .

He stopped himself from engaging in that useless line of thought. That was a phrase that in his estimation should be stricken from the language. It was defeatist and unfailingly futile and he would not allow himself to fall into its snare.

Regrets? No thank you. He must concentrate on pressing ahead.

Why, come the daylight he could travel forward again. Tomorrow might well be the day when he would catch up with Miss Grace and be united with her once more. Proclaim his devotion to her. And, um, explain to her the similarities that bound them as a perfect match. If only she knew . . . Dammit, there was that phrase again. Banish it. Cast it out. Defeatism was not for him, thank you. Forward, ever forward.

He grunted. Swallowed a bit more of the hot yellow water. Very nearly felt the better because of this line of thought.

Something, some animal or other, made a sound in the night, and J. Aubrey felt his moment of good humor dissipate. He was scared to be alone out here. Now that was the simple truth of it.

If only . . .

NINE

THE FIGURE rose up before him like a dark and sinister apparition, a broomstick scarecrow come somehow to life with its twig arms moving and its ragbag clothing hanging limp and tattered.

J. Aubrey yelped and came to his feet, the cup of hot yellow water spilling over his lap and making him yelp a second time. "Don't . . ."

"Whoa now, neighbor." The stick figure grinned and drawled and turned its head and spat.

J. Aubrey felt the pounding in his chest begin to slow and there was hope that his breathing might soon return to normal. "Who . . . ?"

"Th' name's Truly, neighbor. Truly Bokamper?" The Texan, for so J. Aubrey now perceived him to be, put a rising voice inflection on the end of that statement, making it sound like a question even though it was not. "An' who would you be, good neighbor?"

"My, uh . . ."—J. Aubrey regained control of himself—"my name, sir, is J. Aubrey Whitford. Esquire." He managed a smile. "You must forgive me, Mr. Bokamper. I was startled by your, um, unexpected appearance."

"Yeah, I kinda had it in mind that you didn' hear me comin'."

"Um, yes."

Truly Bokamper glanced off toward the patch of thorns that constituted the prairie here, presumably to check upon his horse or horses, then advanced on to stand over J. Aubrey's campfire. "Coffee," he ventured aloud, sniffing. "Now

I hain't tasted coffee in I dunno how long, Aubrey. You did say that was yer handle, didn' you? Aubrey?"

"That is correct, sir. Would you, um, care for a cup of coffee, Mr. Bokamper?"

"Now, Aubrey, ol' friend, it's right neighborly of you t' offer the coffee. I'd be obliged for a taste of it. But do me another favor, Aubrey. Don' be callin' me Mister. Hit confuses me." Truly Bokamper cackled with laughter, as if he'd made a joke. J. Aubrey chuckled along with him for the sake of politeness.

Bokamper seemed a typical Texan all right, J. Aubrey decided, right down to a distressing absence of even the most common social skills.

He looked the part too. Now that his guest was standing closer to the fire J. Aubrey could see that the initial impression of Bokamper as scarecrow hadn't been far off the mark. The man was no heftier of limb than many a hickory tool handle, and his clothing—rags that any discerning housewife would have turned into throw rugs long since—hung loose and floppy about his scrawny person. His homespun trousers were tied round his middle with a length of twine, and his wide-brimmed straw hat looked like goats had already made at least one meal off it. The soles of his boots were secured to the scuffed and filthy uppers by more lengths of crudely sewn twine. Yet the handle of a large knife protruded from one pocket of his britches and the handle of an even larger pistol, or perhaps one of those revolving cylinder arms that the Texans seemed to prefer, extended from the other. Truly Bokamper was an odd figure to have come at one out of the night, J. Aubrey decided.

Bokamper hunkered down beside the fire and picked up J. Aubrey's own cup. Either the man possessed none of his own or did not wish to be bothered with fetching it. Certainly he exhibited no reluctance to make use of another's utensil without first washing it. Bokamper smiled at his host and tilted the pot to pour steaming coffee into the enameled steel mug.

"What the . . . ?"

"Is something wrong, Mr. Bokamper? Truly, that is?"

Bokamper blinked and stared from the cup to J. Aubrey and back again. "I coulda swore I smelt coffee here. What'd you go an' do t' it?"

"Boiled it, of course. That is, I believe, the proper procedure."

Bokamper smelled of the steam rising out of the pot, then tilted it in an attempt to peer inside. With the only available light coming from the fire at ground level it was quite impossible to see into the bottom of any container that was not made of clear glass. Bokamper resolved that difficulty by dumping out J. Aubrey's carefully boiled beverage, pouring it onto the ground without regard for its loss and then spilling the coffee beans out as well.

"See here now," J. Aubrey protested. "If you don't care for it, at least don't waste it. Others might want it even if you don't."

"Waste? Waste what?" Bokamper picked up a bean and examined it. The small, dark, ovoid bean had a skin that was slightly wrinkled but seemed otherwise unaffected by having been boiled. "You done this, Aubrey?"

"Of course."

Bokamper began to grin. And then to laugh. "Mister . . . I know, dammit, you don't need t' be turnin' my own word back ag'in me, but in your case I reckon Mister's in order fer a change . . . Mister, whatever are you a'doin' out here without a keeper?"

It was J. Aubrey's turn to sniff. In this instance, however, that had nothing to do with a desire to smell of anything. It was protest pure and simple, and even a rustic like this Bokamper fellow should be able to comprehend it.

Bokamper laughed again and stood. "C'mon in, boys.

This here fella ain't holding no cards up his sleeve," he said in a low, conversational, perfectly normal sort of voice.

J. Aubrey had no idea what the man was talking about. Nor to whom. Cards? What had cards or gambling to do with anything? The discussion had to do with coffee, did it not? And waste?

Behind him he heard a slight scraping sound and then the soft crunch of gravel underfoot. He turned.

Out of the darkness came two more men, Texans, essentially similar to Truly Bokamper in size and shape and general appearance. The primary difference between Truly and these other two was that the newcomers each held a short-barreled rifle cradled in the crook of his arm.

It occurred to J. Aubrey that if he had been so foolish as to try to harm Bokamper in some fashion . . . He blinked. Some things it is better to refrain from examining with all the vividness of one's imagination.

"C'mere, Aubrey," Truly Bokamper went on, quite as if nothing exceptional were occurring. "First thing you c'n meet m' brothers Tedwell an' Thomas. Next thing, by damn, we're gonna teach you t' mash up them coffee beans a'fore you go an' boil 'em. C'mere an' I'll show you how." He hunkered down beside the fire again.

TEN

THE BOKAMPER BOYS—they were barely distinguishable one from another—were Texas bred, Texas born and Texas raised. And for some reason were proud of it. J. Aubrey Whitford couldn't quite comprehend that last part, if only because Texas seemed to have provided the three of them with almighty little in the way of creature comforts or education or any other civilized form of wealth or accomplishment. Still, they seemed pleasant youngsters and honest enough, wishing no one harm. Thank goodness.

"Y'see, Aubrey, you gotta mash these here beans. You went an' bought some that's a'ready roasted an' that's good. Now you wanta bust 'em up real small, like this." Truly—J. Aubrey was sure of him but tended to become confused sometimes between Tedwell and Thomas—used the butt end of his knife handle to hammer more of J. Aubrey's coffee beans against a flat slab of stone. Actually, J. Aubrey was pretty sure, Truly didn't so much intend a lesson here as another pot of coffee. The Bokamper brothers had already consumed two pots—genuinely excellent the way they made it—and seemed to be about to boil yet another. It was a very good thing indeed that their host had been so recently victualed in Esmeraldaville.

"Y' want me t' show you how t' cook you up some o' this pork?" another Bokamper, possibly Tedwell, most generously offered.

"By all means do," J. Aubrey supplied. If the truth be known he was more than half afraid of these near-savage young men who had the ability to materialize out of thin air. If they were hungry he might be well advised to feed them

lest they think of alternate methods for adding fresh supplies to their own packs.

"I done retied yer stock t' th' picket pins for y', Aubrey,"
the third Bokamper ventured. "You'd'a lost 'em by morning
th' way you had 'em knotted."

"Thank you."

"My pleasure." The boy—it was difficult to guess the ages
of anyone so lank and desiccated as these young men
seemed to be, but late teens to early twenties probably en-
compassed the bunch of them—looked with obvious relish
at the foods that were being pulled out of J. Aubrey Whitford's pack.

"Y' wouldn't happen t' know how t' mix you up some
corn dodgers, would y', Aubrey?" Tedwell asked.

"Perhaps you could teach me?"

All three of the Bokampers grinned.

ELEVEN

"WHERE YOU BOUND, Aubrey?" Tedwell asked. It was morning, at least an hour past the dawning, and J. Aubrey could no longer understand how once he might have had difficulty in discriminating among these delightful young men. Tedwell, Thomas and Truly were, um, truly—he fair blushed at the awfulness of the pun—a joy to have about. Since they'd made their appearance he and his animals were properly tended, all bellies filled and all possible rest obtained. J. Aubrey hadn't had to lift a hand toward his own needs. His part of the bargain, of course, was that the Bokamper boys hadn't had to contribute any provisions. A bargain indeed in J. Aubrey Whitford's view.

"What was that, good fellow?"

"I say where ye bound, Aubrey?"

"Do you mean to ask whither I travel?"

Tedwell frowned. "Uh huh. I reckon."

J. Aubrey explained his mission. In, of course, a slightly edited form such as had been discussed back in Esmeraldaville. That remained close enough to truth for the purposes of the moment.

"Damn, Aubrey. This sister o' yorn. You say she has a beau?"

"I do."

"She pretty?"

"Tedwell!" Truly injected sharply.

"Sorry."

"I take no offense," J. Aubrey assured the boys.

"Good, 'cause we didn't go to offer none."

"None taken."

"Point is, Aubrey, me an' Thomas an' Truly, we're just kinda out on a scout. You know what it is, a scout, Aubrey?"

"I cannot say that I do, Tedwell."

"You mought call it kinda like makin' a ride 'round the country. T' see what there is t' see, like." Tedwell grinned. So did his brothers.

"Just . . . riding willy-nilly about the country?"

"Yeah, kinda like that. See if there's Injuns raidin' or new folks breakin' ground or . . . hell, or most anything else there is t' see."

"And on this scout of yours . . . ?"

"Most interestin' thing we found us so far, Aubrey, is you. What I was thinkin', if'n the notion pleases you, we could kinda ride along with you. He'p you catch up with this sister o' yorn. We got nothin' better t' do, see. An' it'd please us t' he'p you out."

"How extraordinarily kind of you," J. Aubrey declared. He smiled. "I must say, gentlemen, that I have experienced more in the way of human kindness since I landed upon the bleak yet hospitable shores of your Texas than ever before in my entire experience."

"Yeah?"

"I mean that, boys. I truly do."

"What?" Truly asked.

J. Aubrey blinked. Then saw the sly grin that was lurking at the corners of Truly's thin lips and realized that his leg was being tugged on by the eldest Bokamper.

"So what d'you say, Aubrey? You want we should ride along an' help you catch up with your sister?" Thomas persisted.

"Gentlemen," J. Aubrey declared, "I should be delighted, nay more than that, I should be honored if you three Texans would consent to guide me along my way."

Truly and Tedwell and Thomas laughed and yelped and danced a dust-raising celebratory reel, then all scattered to their duties, within moments transforming the camp into nothing more than a patch of beaten earth where not even the coals from the breakfast fire could now be seen. Minutes more and the horses and pack burro were all prepared for travel as well.

Tedwell held the head of J. Aubrey's horse, Thomas held the off stirrup down and Truly Bokamper helped lift the gentleman traveler onto his saddle. This, J. Aubrey realized, was the better way to travel by horseback if travel by horseback he must. He smiled and accepted the assistance as his due, then waited patiently while the Bokampers swung lithely onto their own shaggy ponies.

"North you said she was goin', Aubrey?"

"So I was told, Thomas, yes."

Truly nodded and Tedwell loped away in a direction J. Aubrey would not have suspected of being northward. Thomas nodded to his brother, although no sound or signal had passed between them that J. Aubrey recognized, and trotted off in another direction altogether. Finally Truly himself took up the leash—lead rope—for the burro and motioned for J. Aubrey to follow.

"Jus' keep wipin' that horse's nose on the butt of this 'un, Aubrey, and bye an' bye we'll have you t' your sister again."

J. Aubrey felt considerably better on this morning than he had in some time past. He leaned comfortably back in his saddle—although not so far back that he could no longer reach the knob thing should the ride become shaky—and actually allowed himself to relax a bit while horseback.

TWELVE

J. AUBREY WHITFORD luxuriated in the mingled comforts of warm blankets on a chill morning, coffee hot and fresh in his cup and breakfast warm and satisfying in his stomach.

If a man was forced to camp out then this was the way to do so, he concluded.

For the past three days the faithful Truly, Thomas and Tedwell had been his guides, his companions, his protectors, virtually his mentors in the ways of the wild.

Not, however, that J. Aubrey especially wished to learn the ways of the wild.

Much better to keep things as they were this morning with the Bokamper boys up and doing with the dawn while Squire Whitford lay abed and allowed them to wait on him. Breakfast in bed had been a most cunning touch. J. Aubrey hoped it would become the norm while they traveled.

Although that, he was sure, could not continue indefinitely now.

Surely they soon would catch up with Miss Grace—my, how swiftly the girl could flee; another definite plus in the girl's ledger column, the sort of thing that would be useful in the life they were sure to share just as quickly as he found her—and then the Bokampers could go on about their own affairs—odd, now that he thought on it, how little the youngsters spoke of their own lives and their own home, wherever it might be. J. Aubrey and Miss Grace could return to civilized surroundings for the pursuit of their, um, trade.

Last night they had seen firelight in the distance. Tedwell and Thomas rode out together to investigate that intrusion into the solitude of the prairie. When they returned they said they'd spoken to a hide hunter—whatever one of those supposed to be—and that the hunter had no knowledge of a white woman traveling to the north, neither a girl traveling alone nor any miss traveling in company with others.

J. Aubrey lay now in his bed, ankles crossed and blanket tucked high under his chin, only his head and the one hand that held his coffee cup exposed to the elements, and glanced across the fire toward the three boys who were huddled in close conversation beside his packs of foodstuffs and other supplies, all three of them hunkered in a tight, familial circle hard by the smoldering remains of the breakfast fire.

At that distance he could not overhear what they were saying, but last night they had expressed concerns. Tedwell in particular seemed uncertain that there was a Miss Grace to the north for them to follow and find. It had taken the finest of J. Aubrey's persuasive powers to convince Tedwell that he should press onward.

Now it was Tedwell who once again was doing most of the talking, Thomas who was nodding frequently and only Truly who seemed to dissent from whatever position Tedwell espoused.

Perhaps, J. Aubrey thought, he should once again reassure them on the subject.

Reluctantly he left the comforts of his grass-stem bed and, blanket draped around his shoulders to maintain what warmth he could, meandered in the direction of his friends the Bokamper boys.

". . . shoot the sonuvabitch an' be done with it," Tedwell was saying as J. Aubrey came nearer.

J. Aubrey frowned. Was there a problem with one of the animals? No one had said anything to him about it.

"But what if'n it's true?" Truly was responding.

"Aw, you don't believe that no more'n we do. It's all bullshit, Truly. Ain't you figgered that out yet? It's all horsecrap an' hot air."

"But if it *is* true . . . ?"

"If'n 't'was true then we'd be makin' a mistake. But it ain't, so I say we go ahead an' get 'er over an' done with." Tedwell paused and scratched his crotch. It occurred to J. Aubrey to wonder whether it was in deference to the convenience of such a motion that Texans seemed so fond of the posture known as hunkering. Or was that only an unplanned side benefit?

"Besides," Tedwell went on, "how we gonna explain away them horses an' other trappings we took from that camp yonder? I say we get 't over with here an' now."

"And the woman?" Truly persisted.

"Hail," or so the word sounded, "if'n there's a petticoat up ahead we c'n handle that too. Don't need no formal introduction. Not for what I got in mind anyhow." For a second time Tedwell Bokamper took advantage of proximity and fingered himself. But this time the gesture was not a need to scratch but was a crude and bawdy pat, disgustingly suggestive in its nature.

J. Aubrey blinked and frowned. Truly and Thomas Bokamper laughed.

J. Aubrey found the sound of their laughter rather distasteful.

Surely they couldn't be discussing his own dear . . . no. Of course not.

Still and all.

He cleared his throat loudly, the sound of it as artificial as indeed it truly was. The brothers hadn't noticed him standing here. It seemed quite time that they did. J. Aubrey repeated his frown. Sternly this time.

"See here now . . . ," he commenced.

"We was just talkin' about you, Aubrey," Truly said pleasantly.

"You were?"

"Ayuh. Look, Aubrey, are you *sure* that sister o' yorn is runnin' ahead o' us somewheres?"

"Perfectly certain. The gentlemen at Esmeraldaville assured me that she had passed through their community barely in advance of my own arrival. They said she was traveling north as rapidly as was possible."

"North outa town don't need t' mean north once outa sight," Thomas reminded. It was a notion that was not actually foreign to J. Aubrey's own thoughts and fears. If Grace hadn't continued to the north then all these days might well have been wasted. That was a disquieting thought indeed.

"I say we do it," Tedwell commented, his voice returning J. Aubrey's thoughts and concerns to the here and now instead of moot speculation about Miss Grace's present whereabouts.

"Thomas?" Truly asked.

Thomas nodded.

"That's it then, Aubrey. We done took us a vote, an' my brothers carry th' question two t' one. Sorry, Aubrey."

"Sorry?"

"What it is, Aubrey, we're givin' up on ever catchin' that there purty sister o' yours. Leastways we're givin' up on draggin' you along t' make things easy."

"I don't . . . understand."

"If you work on it, Aubrey, I bet you c'n figger it out." Truly stood. So did Tedwell. So did Thomas.

Tedwell pulled out a knife. J. Aubrey had never seen anything so large nor so bright nor so sharp as the blade of that knife seemed.

Until Truly withdrew his knife. And Thomas displayed his as well.

"Boys?"

"You was nice enough t' share, Aubrey. We'll be nice enough t' handle this quick. Why, you won't hardly feel nary thing."

"You . . . you . . . you. . . ."

"Yeah, I reckon 'tis so, Aubrey," Truly said cheerfully. "Boy, some days you just cain't trust nobody, eh, Aubrey?"

J. Aubrey felt faint. He clutched the blanket tighter to his shoulders, as if that somehow would make him proof against harm, the same sort of silliness that made small boys cover their heads against bumps in the night.

Except this threat was neither ghostie nor goblin.

The Bokamper boys were real.

And they were murderous.

Actually, literally, honestly murderous.

Had they no feeling? No compassion? No sense of honor? No realization that it is guile and not force that determines the worth of any scofflaw worth his salt? Or hers?

Oh, dear Grace.

Once through with him would they pursue Grace still? Would they catch up with her? Abduct her? Abuse her beloved person?

It was not to be permitted. Even the thought of such a heinous crime was not to be permitted.

J. Aubrey steeled himself.

He would fight the dastards if fight he must. He would. . . .

He looked at them again.

Three of them.

Three of them *armed*.

With knives.

Big knives.

Sharp knives.

He could tell they were sharp by the gleam of light reflecting off the cutting edges.

Oh, dear.

Three of them?

J. Aubrey felt his knees sag, felt his resolve quail and tremble before the truth of this awful situation. Felt . . . felt a certain flood of warm moisture within his trousers if the truth be known.

J. Aubrey held his blanket tight to his shoulders.

Tensed himself.

And with a scream on his lips turned and began to gallop madly across the prairie with the blanket flapping and thrashing about his limbs.

Behind him there were more screams. Of rage? Of pursuit? He knew not. Only that he was screaming. The Bokampers were screaming. For a moment there it seemed that all the banshees and hoodoos of the netherworld were screaming as well.

J. Aubrey heard the sounds of the screaming.

Tripped.

Fell.

Crashed hard onto the thorn-studded earth, and was encapsulated within a dark and floating void.

He knew no more.

THIRTEEN

"UHHH MMNMH GRUH."

It made sense to him at the time although a moment later it had no meaning whatsoever.

J. Aubrey groaned. And blinked. Oh, God, he thought. I'm blind. Or dead. Was dying like this? No, dammit, he was alive. He had to be. Surely it wouldn't hurt so awfully bad when you were dead. Death and pain at one and the same time would be simply too cruel to contemplate.

So he was alive. But blind. He groaned again, not immediately sure if that trade-off was worthwhile. That is . . . well . . . of course it was good to be alive. But damn. . . .

He tried to rub at his eyes and discovered that his hands wouldn't move. They felt numb but when he attempted to move them they tingled and commenced to throb. The sensation was an odd one and decidedly disagreeable. Not only did he want to rub his eyes, now his nose had begun to itch. He needed to scratch it and could not. Most annoying. Most unpleasant. He sneezed, loudly, and at that point became completely convinced that he was indeed clinging to life. Pain after death perhaps, but sneezing? No, he thought not, thank you.

He cleared his throat and wriggled about a bit. His hands seemed to be pinioned behind and beneath his supine person. How very strange. And while he could see nothing, his sense of smell was undiminished. And at the moment was undergoing assault. He was surrounded by scent. By scent? By stink, actually. The area about him was redolent with thick, heavy, quite unidentifiable odors. He wrinkled his nose and sneezed again.

"So. You awake, eh, white man?" The voice was not a familiar one. It was graveled and almost husky yet high-pitched, definitely none of the familiar Bokamper tones. J. Aubrey was positive he had never heard this man speak before now.

"Who are you?" he queried. "Where are you? My apologies, sir, but I find that I am blind. Have you rescued me? What became of—"

"Eh. Shut up, white man. You shut up now."

J. Aubrey bristled, at least insofar as he was able under these awkward circumstances. "Come now, sir. There is no need for you to become cheeky, you know. One can be civil whilst—" His complaint was interrupted, and effectively terminated, by a blow stoutly delivered to the side of his head. He yelped.

"I tell you shut up, you shut up. You hear me, white man?"

J. Aubrey cleared his throat. He glared in the direction whence came the voice.

"You frown to me, white man? Tha's all right, eh? You shut up so tha's all right." The voice snickered. Unpleasant SOB, J. Aubrey thought. To himself. "You wanta sit up now, white man?"

He nodded.

A hand grasped his shoulder and pulled, drawing him into a sitting position. "That is much better, thank you."

The odd voice said something in a gibberish language J. Aubrey could not comprehend. Then, "So, white man, you hungry?"

"No," he responded before he took time to think about the question. After all, he'd just finished his breakfast, hadn't he? Well, hadn't he? He had. He was sure that he had. Yet after a moment's contemplation he realized that indeed he was hungry. And his bladder was uncomfortably full even though . . . the point was that his trousers felt dry now and his bladder refilled. Just how much time had passed since the Bokamper brothers attempted to kill him? For that matter, what happened to thwart them? Where were they? And how was he rendered blind? So many questions. So much as yet unknown. "See here now," he began in a loudly querulous tone.

"You shut you up, white man, or I will tell my friends to go ahead an' take your scalp, eh? They do that if I tell them to. *Before* they kill you. You think 'bout that."

J. Aubrey shuddered. And once more shut up.

He heard movement. More voices, all in the language he did not understand. One thing he did understand now was that he was surrounded by Indians. Scalped, the voice in English had said. That meant that Indians had him. J. Aubrey began to tremble. It couldn't honestly be said that he would rather remain in the clutches of the Bokampers. Not considering what their intentions had been. But . . . Indians . . . ? He felt sweat accumulate around the crown of his head and begin to trickle over his temples and down his neck.

"Here, white man. You eat now." He felt hands picking and pulling at the back of his head and a moment later realized that his face was constricted by the application of a binding device that now was being removed. A blindfold! That was all that was wrong with his eyes. Thank goodness.

The mask-like strip of soft leather dropped away, taking some of the stink with it, and J. Aubrey blinked in the sudden brightness. Brightness relative to complete dark, that is. In truth the interior of this strange structure would not otherwise have seemed bright at all. In fact, under normal circumstances, dark and fetid and gloomy would have been a charitable conclusion about the charms of the place. Wherever it was.

The place where J. Aubrey now found himself was something akin to the inside of a monstrously huge dunce cap. An inverted cone sort of thing. But twenty, perhaps twenty-five feet in diameter. And made of soft fabric—no, soft leather he saw upon further inspection—soft leather that was supported by a mass of wooden poles arranged in a circle. No, not exactly in a circle, he saw. More like an elliptical pattern. If it mattered. Which he was sure it did not.

The floor of this odd place was carpeted with small rugs that proved actually to be the hairy skins of dead animals.

Beaded and feathered and gaudily decorated items of savage creation and incomprehensible purpose hung from various of the support poles within this structure. J. Aubrey peered intently from one of these to another and back again, unsure of what he intended but determined to carry out his search with grim resolution. Still trembling, he tried to concentrate his attention on the objects that surrounded him. Oh, God, he thought, his breathing coming swift and shallow now.

"So, white man. You not hungry? You sure?"

That was what he was trying to ignore, of course.

The people.

He was surrounded.

He was . . . frightened. Petrified was more properly descriptive. And now all his attempts to escape reality by ignoring it came crashing down.

He *was* surrounded. And they *were* painted savages.

All right, not painted. Not at the moment anyway. But they were greased and grimy enough that it seemed hardly worth quibbling over. They might as well have been painted.

There were . . . there were—his breath caught in his throat and a small whimper escaped his lips as he recognized the enormity of the threat that surrounded him—there were at least a dozen of the ugly savages gathered inside this upside-down tent thing.

They were . . . they were—he groaned, became conscious of a thousand prickling itches—they were all staring at him. Intently. Maliciously. He was sure he could see a blood-crazed madness in each and every eye that was pointed his way.

There were at least a dozen of them and all but two were men, he saw now.

The men sat cross-legged on the skin rugs, gathered round a fire that burned in the middle of the tent, or they reclined against seat-back things that looked like willow withe chairs fashioned with no legs. Crazy, savage implements of some sort, no doubt. J. Aubrey shivered again. At the moment he would have welcomed seeing a pack of Texans in their odd, hunkering posture, instead of these stern-faced Indians who sat with unblinking, darkly glowering expressions. Oh, dear. Oh, goodness.

The men wore breechclouts and leather leggings, some of them with vests and a few with filthy coats but most of them bare-chested. Their hair was long and braided and shiny with grease. Firelight glittered and glinted in the dark, gleaming pools of hate that were their eyes. The sight was enough to give J. Aubrey chills.

The women—there were only the two, one tending to something in a pot on the central fire and the other kneeling quite close at J. Aubrey's side—wore dirty and unkempt but otherwise fairly ordinary dresses. It occurred to J. Aubrey— not that he really much cared in this particular time and place—that the stories he'd been told about Indian women not bothering to cover themselves were proven false here.

Only one of the women, the one by the fire, had the same coloration and facial features as the Indian men. The woman who was kneeling close to him was no darker than the rest, but her features were those of a Negress rather than an Indian. Or so he thought. J. Aubrey had seen Negroes before, of course. But awfully few Indians. He could have been mistaken.

Not that any of it mattered.

Nothing, absolutely nothing, would possibly matter here if the ultimate purpose of these frightening savages was to murder him in cold blood. Indians did that, didn't they? He was sure they did. Although to what purpose he was unclear. They simply went about slaughtering everything and everyone they encountered. That was what was said of them. Everyone knew it. That was what Indians did. They murdered and pillaged and destroyed without conscience. Except when . . .

Sweet Jesus in heaven above.

He went cold, chilled to his very core and frozen into shocked immobility.

In Texas . . . it was said . . . there were certain tribes of savages . . . who were . . . cannibals.

Oh, God!

Is that why his life had thus far been spared?

The sweat that already coursed across his face turned as icy as water fresh-issued from a mountain spring.

J. Aubrey began to feel faint.

The Negress at his side grunted and plucked something, some sort of meat dripping with juices, out of a bowl she held cupped in the palm of her dark hand. She grunted again and thrust it toward his mouth. "Eat now, white man."

He scarcely registered the fact that the gravelly "man's" voice belonged to the Negress. His total concentration was on the meat she held out toward him.

Were these people wanting to make him plump?

Or only to taunt him?

Was this . . . could it be . . . was he being offered some selected portion of roast Bokamper?

J. Aubrey felt his stomach heave. But before he had time enough to evacuate his churning belly the awful implications of his predicament closed in around him, and he returned to the blessed oblivion of a dead and total faint.

FOURTEEN

J. AUBREY reluctantly returned to consciousness only to feel chill sweat accumulating on his neck and coursing down onto his chest. Then it occurred to him that the moisture he was feeling was not sweat but some sort of cool, laving liquid that was being applied to his cheeks and brow by way of a cloth. He could feel too then that someone seemed to be propping him into a semi-upright position. Odd. He cleared his throat and immediately the person who was supporting him moved to mop his forehead once again.

"You all right now, white man?" It was the Negress. "Here." She set her damp cloth aside and for a second time thrust a bite of juicy meat at him. This time he was unprepared for the assault. She caught him unawares and succeeded in forcing the warm morsel between his lips as if she were feeding a recalcitrant infant.

J. Aubrey gagged. But couldn't help from noticing that the meat tasted remarkably like roast beef. Not that he had any idea what braised Bokamper might be like. But even so. . . . "What, uh, is that? If I may be so bold as to ask."

The woman gave him a questioning look. "Cow. What you think?"

J. Aubrey chose not to answer.

"You want more?"

He nodded. She plucked another bite-sized piece from a woven willow platter-like thing on the ground at her side and fed it to him. It was really quite good beef, J. Aubrey conceded. "I think I can sit up on my own now, thank you."

She shrugged and gave him a push. "You wanta feed yourself too, white man?"

"That would be fine, thank you."

The woman turned and said something to the savages who surrounded them, her comments drawing a round of laughter. Then she got up and walked away, stepping over to the slanting leather wall and following it around to the far side of the tent structure although it would have been shorter and simpler for her to walk directly there past the fire in the center. She paused to engage in a brief conversation with an elderly, gray-haired Indian who was seated there, then settled herself onto a pile of huge, dark brown shaggy skins behind the old man.

J. Aubrey reached for the plate of meat that had been offered.

Or tried to. He had quite forgotten for the moment that his hands remained tied behind his back. That must have been what the Indians were laughing about a moment earlier. Damn them.

"Miss? I say . . . you there."

The Negress yawned, sat upright on the pile of skins long enough to peel her dress off over her head, not seeming to care in the slightest that she was exposing herself to the view of all in the place—although for that matter no one else seemed to care very much either; certainly no one bothered to stare in her direction despite her state of undress—and slid beneath the topmost skin like someone who was going to bed.

"Here now, you can't leave me like this," J. Aubrey protested.

The only reaction he got was a hooded glower from several of the younger savages who were seated in the circle close to the old man who J. Aubrey presumed was the leader of this band.

The other woman finished whatever task she had been about, disappeared outdoors for a time and then returned to go to bed on another pile of skins close to that already occupied by the Negress. The male Indians talked among themselves for a time, their voices becoming softer and lower as the fire burned lower and became glowing coals rather than illuminating flame. Eventually they all either left or went to bed, the old man sharing the Negress's skin pallet.

J. Aubrey sat where he was. Ignored. Which, he concluded, was somewhat better than things might have been. He decided to accept it as a good sign and eventually he too put himself to bed, in his case this requiring only that he topple sideways from a sitting to a recumbent posture.

Savage Indians, he discovered, snore. Whoever would have guessed it?

After a time he was able to sleep.

FIFTEEN

MORNING FOUND HIM stiff and sore and frightfully thirsty. And there were certain other discomforts as well, matters that required the use of his own hands and a small amount of privacy.

"Good morning," he said politely when the Negress arose. There were Indians sleeping all about the tent floor, but the dark-skinned woman was the first to waken and stir.

"G'morning, white man."

"Would you, um . . . that is, if you wouldn't mind. . . ." He turned, pointedly presenting his bound wrists toward her.

"Ha, I know what you need. Know what you want too. Go ahead if you think you fast enough. Or brave enough."

"Pardon?"

"You wanta run away, white man, you go ahead an' try, hey. Eh, who knows, maybe you get away."

"That wasn't at all what I had in mind." And indeed it was not. The possibility of escape by fleetness of foot simply hadn't occurred to him.

"No? So you think about it. Make things easy, eh? Stop all this fuss-fuss-fuss. Go ahead. You run away. I won't say nothing."

"Fuss? What fuss?"

While she talked the woman—mercifully, in J. Aubrey's opinion—knelt behind him and unfastened the bonds. "Them Injun, they fuss, you know. Back an' forth, back an' forth. Can't make up they minds. Dumb damn Injuns. Can't figure do they wanta take you scalp or sell you to them white so'jers."

J. Aubrey sputtered and coughed as a surge of fear shot through him like a bolt of sizzling lightning. "Scalp?"

"Sure. Hey, what you think?"

"But. . . ."

The woman laughed, stood, took him by the elbow and helped him to his feet. He tottered there, not at all steady and feeling distinctly unwell in light of this unexpected information.

"What you think?" she repeated as she guided him outside into the pale light of a chill dawning. "You think them Injun save you from getting killed on purpose? Ha. Why they wanta do that, huh? We riding along minding our own business, see, going home after raid . . . got them nice horses you see there an' took some cow meat, right? . . . riding along, mind our own business. Then we see these white men gonna shoot somebody. You. Except you, you're wearing damn blanket, eh? Look like some Injun. So them warriors, they come help. Wouldn't'a done that if they'd knowed you another damn white man." She frowned, spat, shook her head. "Now they got you, what t' hell they gonna do with you? That's the fuss-fuss-fuss."

"I, um, have a suggestion," J. Aubrey offered.

"Hey, I bet you do, ain't it?" the Negress said with a grin. "Over there, eh? That's the place you want." The woman hadn't sensibility enough to turn her head. And J. Aubrey hadn't the physical capacity to wait her out. He tended to what was necessary and tried not to think about having an audience.

"You sure you don' wanta run?" she mused, picking up a spear of grass and chewing on it. "Make things easier if you run. No need to think then. If they catch you they scalp you. If you get away you get away. Simple, yes?"

"Really, miss, I believe we should discuss this before any rash decisions are made." J. Aubrey rubbed his hands together and even managed a smile. He was feeling somewhat better now. Considerably better, in fact. At least he understood now what was happening.

That, he concluded, had to be at least half the battle.

"What did you say your name was, pretty lady?" he inquired as they strolled, he leading the way this time, back toward the tent.

SIXTEEN

J. AUBREY elicited the woman Jeptha's life story and listened to it—amid sympathetic clucks and appropriately placed mutterings—while he wolfed down the cold remains of the beef he had been unable to feed himself the night before. The plate of food had been left on the floor overnight.

Jeptha was, unsurprisingly, a runaway former slave. Brought to Missouri as a child, she had no concept of whence she came. No conscious memory of parents or homeland, no notion whether she might have been born on American soil or elsewhere. She knew only that she was born into servitude and was expected to docilely accept that condition as her appointed lot.

Jeptha was, surprisingly or not depending upon one's own perceptions of "the peculiar institution," unappreciative of the benefits inherent in her status. Even as a girl she proved incapable of comprehending the great good fortune of security, provision, shelter and clothing, all that was given freely to her whilst she in turn never once had to worry herself with the minutiae of life's decisions. But then some people never know when they are well off.

She was still a girl when her master journeyed from Missouri to Santa Fe, taking Jeptha with him to serve as his cook and body servant.

Unappreciative Jeptha parted company from the train of ox-drawn wagons somewhere on the dry and barren prairie that is crossed by the Santa Fe Trail. She slipped away in the night, she explained, and at the earliest opportunity presented herself in the first Indian encampment she saw. She had been with them ever since. Of her own free will. As an equal. She snorted loudly when she said that, flaring her nostrils in defiance of fate and tossing her head proudly. "Good as any-damn-body you betcha," she declared.

"Right as rain," J. Aubrey seconded firmly. "I could not agree more. How, um, long ago has all this been?" he asked.

Jeptha frowned in concentration for several moments, then shrugged. "I dunno. Twen'y years. More, I think. What comes after twen'y?"

J. Aubrey didn't bother to answer. The number was obviously moot. After the passage of so very much time there would be no reward outstanding for Jeptha's return. Not, of course, that he would have undertaken such an endeavor even if he had been in a position to do so. Of course not. But it was impossible to avoid *thinking* about it. He cleared his throat and squirmed a bit on the furry mat that served as a chair within the aboriginal tent. Lodge, Jeptha called it. "You don't have any more of this beef, do you?" He plucked the last morsel off the woven platter and tried to hand it back to Jeptha for a refill. She ignored him and after a moment he set the platter aside still empty.

The Indians who also slept in this tent—lodge—were awake now and commencing their day's activities. The other woman had rekindled the fire in the center of the lodge and was preparing a thick stew of sorts in a small copper kettle, dumping in water and chunks of slimy, purple meat and some sort of dried, powdery substance obtained from an oiled leather case. The resulting mess looked revolting. It smelled wonderful. J. Aubrey began to salivate. The bits of leftover beef had been too few to fully assuage his hunger.

The Indian men were going about their morning routines. Combing and oiling and braiding their hair. Examining themselves for body lice . . . and depositing the fruits of these labors into the fire where they sizzled and occasionally popped. Using crude tweezers to pluck facial hairs, which seemed a terribly uncomfortable substitute for an ordinary shave. J. Aubrey winced at the thought of it. He rubbed a palm over his own lengthening beard stubble and hoped his hosts did not insist that he adopt their methods of depilation.

The men's careful attention to their persons surprised him. He would not have expected it of savages such as these. What surprised him the more was the playful nature of their banter as they did the things they were doing.

Not that J. Aubrey could understand a word of it. Not one. But the tone was familiar enough. Nudges, jibes and chuckles, even the occasional prank was evident. Apart from the oddity of language and the detail of the men's actions, this might well have been J. Aubrey's own little band of adventurers so recently left behind on their journey to Baja California. It amazed him to discover that these savages seemed so like those civilized travelers.

Then one of the Indians turned to give J. Aubrey a look and said something to the fellow who was squatting at his side. This second man laughed and nudged another, obviously repeating what the first had said. All three seemed to get a kick out of the statement. Whatever it had been. All three of them stared for a moment at their captive and then, all of them together, laughed evilly.

Whatever was said, J. Aubrey was quite sure he did not care for it. There was something in the tone of the laughter that was ominously sinister and threatening. He recalled Jeptha's conversation earlier and felt a prickling sensation commence at the nape of his neck and tingle its way forward across his scalp.

J. Aubrey cleared his throat and looked away, pretending not to have noticed the trio of savages.

And savages they were, he concluded now. Never mind any supposed similarities with civilized human beings. These Indians might yet determine to coldly murder him and then celebrate their savagery by slicing off portions of his person for trophies.

The idea was enough to make him feel faint, and he was glad that he hadn't had more to eat than he did.

"You all right, white man? You gonna be sick or somethin'?" Jeptha's voice reached him as if from a great distance. It sounded thin and tinny, and there was a high-pitched buzzing in his ears.

"Fine. Yes, of course fine," he insisted. He was, however, frantically trying to think of something . . . some ruse or plan or . . . or just anything at all that would allow him to escape these terrifying savages. He felt sweat gather on his neck and run cold within his shirt collar, but he ignored that minor discomfort and tried to concentrate on the task at hand. On, that is, the task of survival.

SEVENTEEN

"YOU KNOW," he mused aloud, "I'm beginning to feel frightfully like a jinx."

Jeptha said nothing. But she was close by. He was sure she was listening.

"Kidnapped twice now. How utterly amazing. For one person to have been kidnapped twice . . . incomprehensible, astounding. Those men from whom you people, um, rescued me. They'd kidnapped me too, you understand. The white men, that is. Had I mentioned that? No? Well, they had. It was an unconscionable act, of course. Good riddance to them, I say. Whatever you did with them. Not that I am, ahem, asking. Not at all. As for this band of stalwart souls, why, I have nothing but the best of will and the deepest of gratitude." He paused, blinked, tried to assess Jeptha's expression to see if he might be making some small impression upon her. He simply couldn't tell.

"I am a man of no small substance. As you may well appreciate. Not a slaveholder, though. No, I am from New York. Have you been there? Wonderful city. I miss it terribly." Well, *that* was true enough. "Not a slave state, New York. New Yorkers as a rule—I speak of the dwellers in the city now, you understand—are great leaders of the libertarian movements. Wonderful folk, New Yorkers. Always eager to lend a helping hand to others. Very much in the forefront of the quest for liberty and dignity for all mankind. It was only necessity that forced me to leave, I assure you." That too was true, the necessity in question having been a gentleman with a firearm and a wrathful disposition, something to do with his errant wife. Nonsense for him to have thought it J. Aubrey's fault if the woman strayed, of course. But it hadn't seemed advisable to debate the point at that particular moment in time.

J. Aubrey sighed heavily. Fate. So fickle. So untrustworthy. If it hadn't been for those unpleasant events he should still be in the city where genuinely civilized comforts could be found. On the other hand, if it hadn't been for that same unfortunate twist of fate he never would have made the acquaintance of Miss Grace. But if he hadn't met Miss Grace he would not now be captive in this squalid lodge of bloodthirsty savages. And if . . .

He grunted. That sort of run-in-circles thinking was enough to give one a headache.

Besides, he had things to do now. Important things.

He feigned a yawn, stretched hugely, smacked his lips and shifted position a mite. Was the woman Jeptha following his motions? He couldn't be sure.

"You know, I should think my companions would be most anxious to see me brought safely back from the harm those scoundrels intended. They would be most appreciative. I would see to it myself, in fact. If, say, I were to be escorted safely to a town or an army post, whichever." He smiled.

Jeptha went on with what she was doing.

"Not a ransom, mind. But a gift freely given." His smile became even broader. He could feel sweat on his forehead but ignored it. "I daresay I would be *most* appreciative if that were to happen."

Jeptha scratched her armpit and coughed.

No matter. It was worth the attempt. J. Aubrey rambled on in that same vein for some little time without ever once attracting the obvious attention of the woman Jeptha or any of the men in the lodge.

EIGHTEEN

AH, THIS WAS MORE like it. Never mind the slow-witted female. One of the men was finally taking note of the band's, um, guest. As the Indian brave marched forward with what seemed a quite customary scowl, J. Aubrey preened a bit in preparation to receive his due. Damned Jeptha. She should have been paying attention long since. It was about time one of the men displayed wit enough to correct the situation.

As the Indian came near J. Aubrey rose to his feet and brushed hastily at his lapels. That was the sum of the sartorial improvement that was open to him under these strained circumstances. He *did* wish that he had his hat, though. First quality silk. Or near enough to it that no one could tell the difference without close inspection. J. Aubrey was particular about his hat, but he hadn't seen it since . . . well . . . since his *rescue* from the Bokampers. No matter. No matter if now this entire, unfortunate situation were to be alleviated. "My *good* man . . . ," J. Aubrey began.

The scowling Indian scowled some more and gestured toward the door of the tent. Lodge, Jeptha called it.

J. Aubrey smiled. "Ah, yes," he said loudly. "And with my thanks, sir. With my deep and undying thanks. I appreciate the rescue. I appreciate your releasing me this way. But might I trouble you as to the whereabouts of my horse and saddle? I shall need them so as to speed back to, um, civilization and, uh, arrange for your reward. Which shall, sir, be ample. I assure you of that. Ample." His smile became broader even as the Indian's scowl deepened.

The Indian reached out and gave him a shove, propelling

him in the direction of the low doorway opening. If he hadn't ducked in time he would have run face first into the leather lining that was hung around the circular walls of the lodge.

"There is no need for you to be rude," J. Aubrey complained. He also beat a hasty retreat through the tent flap to the out-of-doors beyond.

The scowling Indian followed. So did Jeptha. So did several of the other male Indians. J. Aubrey thought the rest of them looked amused. He could not for the life of him imagine why.

The Indian said something.

"I fear you shall have to try English, old fellow," J. Aubrey informed him pleasantly.

This time the Indian fairly snapped.

J. Aubrey shrugged.

The Indian pushed him. J. Aubrey reeled backward, nearly losing his balance. "See here now, my good man. No need for any of that, I say."

The Indian pointed. Off onto the prairie somewhere. J. Aubrey looked. He saw no saddled horse waiting for him in that direction.

"You shall simply have to state your wishes in plain English," he said amicably. "I am afraid I must insist on it."

Those first scowls had been nothing compared to this. Now the Indian looked positively murderous.

As if to reinforce that most unpleasant impression, the savage actually drew a knife from a decorated scabbard thing slung at his waist.

"Hey!" J. Aubrey yelped.

"He want you to pick up chip for fire," Jeptha commented from her position of observation by the lodge.

"Chip? Wood shavings, you mean? I see no chips here, dammit. And besides, I really must be on my way soon. Can't tarry, you understand. I have to go arrange for the reward to be paid to this, um, band of heroes who rescued me." He attempted a smile but was fairly sure the attempt was less than successful.

"Chip," Jeptha repeated. And explained.

"You want me . . . me? . . . to pick up . . . that? With my *hands?*"

Jeptha shrugged. And grinned. The scowling Indian scowled. And raised his knife blade as if ready to slice something.

"Buffalo chips. Yes, indeed," J. Aubrey said hastily.

He heard a tittering of laughter at his back, and his ears began to burn.

None of that seemed important, however. He scuttled forward and began anxiously scanning the surface of the ground for the dried dung that Jeptha swore was known as chips. And swore as well could be used as fuel in the absence of wood.

This entire matter was depressingly uncivilized. J. Aubrey moaned quietly to himself as he gathered the first of what would prove to be many armloads of dried buffalo dung. Chips, that is.

NINETEEN

J. AUBREY was not sure if he were more exhausted or more depressed. The question was in doubt.

It was evening. He was miserably tired and hungry to boot, and it was beginning to seem that these savages intended to murder him by way of overwork. All day long he had been trudging back and forth, gathering mountains of buffalo chips and more mountains of dried grass twists. Now the buffalo chips were rapidly being consumed by roaring fires—had the savages no sense of conservatism in such matters? but then obviously not; after all they had no need to go and gather more fuel themselves—and the grass twists were being distributed in massive amounts to serve as bedding.

There were, it seemed, a great many more Indians in the band than J. Aubrey had previously suspected. During the day the first small group had been joined by others until by now surely the entire tribe was assembled. There were a dozen or more of the tents—lodges; as if it mattered what the ugly things were called—and a hundred or more people —which gave a hint as to the uncivilized way in which wild Indians cohabited—and more horses than one would want to try and count.

Half of one horse was now suspended over the fire J. Aubrey had so unwillingly provided. The unfortunate beast had been quite grievously wounded before it was selected for dispatch and was converted from transportation to dinner. J. Aubrey was not sure, one horse looking much like any other, but he found this one vaguely familiar. A mount one of the Bokamper brothers had been riding? He was not sure. And was not sure that he wanted to become sure. This entire situation was becoming simply too, too much to bear.

It was particularly unbearable to think how marvelously good the roasting horse was beginning to smell. Just how far had he sunk, anyway?

A pair of half-naked savages walked by, and one of them looked at him and said something—something snide, no doubt—to the other and then both laughed.

J. Aubrey pretended not to have noticed.

It was impossible for him to not notice, however, when another clutch of the dastards came past him with one tall, potbellied, louse-ridden example of the miserable breed prancing about in the center of attention.

It was too much.

The bloody bugger was wearing J. Aubrey Whitford's own fine hat.

Too, too much.

He squeezed his eyes tight closed and clenched his hands into fists and wished he could just . . . pummel them. Every blasted one of them.

He stood—he'd been sitting silently off to one side in the hope that quiet immobility would serve as a form of camouflage—and began seeking the woman Jeptha, who despite her many failings as an ally at least had the advantage of communication. She was, after all, the only one he had yet found who was intelligent enough to comprehend simple English, all the rest of them being limited to grunts and growls and the like.

TWENTY

JEPTHA and another woman were hunkered close to the fire circle inside the lodge. For the first time since he was so unwillingly introduced into these surroundings, J. Aubrey saw the lodge nearly empty of humans, there being in it now only Jeptha and one Indian woman and the old man. J. Aubrey thought this second woman a newcomer to the group and not the same one he had seen previously. This one must have been off with the warriors who'd shown up during the day. She and Jeptha were like a pair of hens, cackling and belching or whatever it was they did to make the sounds that passed for language here. They were squatting side by side and pawing through the contents of a pair of handsome leather saddlebags. Loot stolen from some unfortunate soul, no doubt.

The woman Jeptha saw J. Aubrey enter the lodge and motioned for him to come near. She took up a flat tin and held it out to him. "What is this, eh?"

J. Aubrey sniffed. The woman was clearly illiterate. The contents of the tin were written plain as plain could be amid red and yellow curlicues painted on the lid. "Sardines," he said. "Trident of Poseidon Brand First Quality Cold Water Sardines, Packed in the Finest Oils Obtainable, None Better Anywhere, Quality Guaranteed, D. K. Wallington Company, East Lynn, Massachusetts."

Jeptha's brow wrinkled. "I ask you what this is, hey. Not all that whatever-you-say."

"Fish," J. Aubrey said.

"Huh." This time her nose wrinkled as she made a sour face and translated for the benefit of the Indian woman. The

Indian woman looked at the sardine can as though it was
something foul—she hadn't room to sneer was J. Aubrey's
opinion; after all, he had seen some of the loathsome things
that these people would put into a stew pot—and Jeptha
tossed the unwanted sardines back into the saddlebag.

She extracted a small purse from the bags next. The thing
was a snap purse, one of those patent devices fashioned
cunningly over a spring steel clip that remains shut unless it
is squeezed on the ends. Once the women discovered how
the purse opened they seemed quite excited by it, both of
them opening and closing it repeatedly while they jabbered
and gestured at one another. Eventually the Indian woman
claimed the purse. She cackled in triumph and held it up for
fond examination. Then, incredibly, she squeezed the
mouth open and upended the container, spilling its contents
into the ashes of the fire circle. The purse had held several
coins. Several bright *yellow* coins, J. Aubrey was quick to
notice. Gold coins. Small denominations, true, but nonetheless. . . . The specie was allowed to tumble unheeded into
the ashes while the leather pouch was retained as a treasure.
J. Aubrey fair winced at the stupidity of these ignorant Children of Nature.

Jeptha, meanwhile, was peering at the next object to be
extracted from the saddlebags. She said something to the
Indian woman and then to the old headman, who was re-
clining on his pile of smelly robes at the rear of the lodge.
The old man responded and looked at the thing she was
showing him, which proved to be a folded newspaper.

Surely the Indian headman could read no better than
Jeptha was able. Could he? J. Aubrey's assumption was confirmed when the headman jerked his chin in J. Aubrey's
direction and said something. Jeptha nodded and stood, carrying the newspaper to J. Aubrey and shoving it beneath his
nose.

"What is this, white man?"

Their consternation became clear. They had been looking

at a woodcut scene on the page, the artist depicting a hideously painted savage clutching his breast whilst in the process of falling to his well-earned demise—well earned, at least, in J. Aubrey's opinion; he doubted that view would be shared by Jeptha and her unpleasant companions—said savage being at that very moment riddled with bullets from the revolving pistols of three dashing horsemen. The artist's drawing showed the horsemen wearing broad-brimmed sombreros and large spurs and carrying several pistols in their sashes. The horsemen quite certainly had to be Texans, J. Aubrey concluded. The type was instantly recognizable.

"What do you mean, what is this?" he inquired. "I should think that would be obvious, even to . . . never mind. I should think it obvious what the picture represents."

"No, you . . . ," and she said something in the strange tongue that he was likely better off not understanding at the moment. "I mean what is this saying. Here." She stabbed a cracked and filthy fingernail onto the line of gray text printed beneath the woodcut.

"Fighting Texans of the Ranging Companies' . . . mmm . . . give me a moment to make this out, will you?"

"You can't read, white man?"

J. Aubrey tipped his chin up and his nose into the air. "Better than you, I daresay."

Jeptha grunted.

"I can read it for you, of course. I assume you want a close and careful rendering of the information?"

"Yeah, sure."

"Then I suggest you allow me time to undertake the effort, uh, properly." He smiled. And held a hand out.

If he were busy perusing a newspaper at the behest of the tribal headman, dammit, it seemed unlikely he would be called upon by any of the others to fetch and carry for them. He had had quite enough of that, thank you.

So why waste a perfectly good opportunity for leisure.

"Hokay," Jeptha consented. She relinquished the newspaper into his care and turned to the headman to explain.

There remained a little daylight in the sky. J. Aubrey carried the newspaper to the door flap and settled himself cross-legged on the earthen floor beside it, angling the newspaper—it proved to have been printed in a place called Austin, in Texas that was, and printed quite recently too according to the date, August 18, 1852, only a matter of a week or so past if he was remembering the current date with any degree of accuracy—so as to better catch the fading sunlight.

Then ignoring the woodcut and its accompanying caption for the time being, J. Aubrey Whitford began reading the entire edition of the *Austin Enterprise* word by word.

TWENTY-ONE

IT HAD BEEN J. Aubrey's intent to read the newspaper front to back and word for word or at least until the light failed to such an extent that he could read no more.

He wasn't halfway through the front page, however, before his eyes became wide and a smile crept across his distinguished features.

He shifted from side to side in considerable agitation and nervously eyed Jeptha seated across the lodge near the old man.

His question now was how much, or how little, the one time slave retained of her scanty knowledge of civilization.

How much knowledge. And how much awe. If any.

She hadn't been swayed by comments about ransom. But then J. Aubrey had already seen how shabbily these silly savages viewed money. Imagine, throwing gold coins away and keeping a purse. Incredible. Yet he'd seen it with his own eyes. No wonder his suggestions about ransom payment failed to strike the necessary chord.

Which reminded him. Sooner or later he really did need to create some excuse to go near the fire. Adding fuel to it, perhaps. That should work. He would volunteer to go out and fetch in fresh chips and add them to the fire. After all, the Indians did not want the gold but that seemed no excuse for allowing the stuff to lie there and be lost.

Ah, but that was merely a side issue of no real importance.

The real question was whether Jeptha retained any amount of respect for her superiors. Whether, in fact, she recognized that she had superiors. Which seemed somewhat in doubt amongst these strange creatures, who had a headman but who seemed to accept little or no direction from him.

Yes, that was the real question.

If gold would not work, might awe be used in its stead? That was what it really came down to.

But then: Nothing ventured, nothing gained. The homily seemed certainly to apply here.

J. Aubrey smiled faintly and once again bent to read the article that had so captured his imagination.

Russian Prince To Visit, the headline read. Sportsman Prince Plans Mountain Adventure. Hunting Guides Prepare For Arrival.

Ha! J. Aubrey thought happily. Indeed, ha.

And commenced to read the article for a third time.

TWENTY-TWO

"CAN I RELY upon your discretion, my good woman?"

"You can get your nose out o' my ear an' set up straight, that's what you can do, white man. Can't nothing you tell me be said where all don't hear. An' besides, can't none o' them make out a word o' English. I'm the only one."

"Yes, um, as you wish."

"One more thing, white man."

"And that would be?"

"Don't you be calling me *your* woman. I'm my *own* woman here, an' don't you never forget it."

He smiled calmly. "But of course. Ahem. I wish to share a confidence with you, my dear wo . . . that is to say, um . . . with you, dear lady."

She grunted. But remained where she was, in a posture of mild interest. Both of them were seated cross-legged beside the door flap. Beyond the leather tenting material night had fallen, and now the lodge was beginning to fill with Indians seated and Indians standing and Indians passing in and out. Loud voices outside proved there remained much activity around the fire ring also.

"What I intend to convey to you, Jeptha, has to remain secret, you see. A matter of personal freedom, which I am sure you can appreciate as few others might."

She lifted an eyebrow but didn't ask anything.

"You see, Jeptha, I too have spent a lifetime doing the bidding of others. Although my chains have been spun of gold and crystal, dear lady, I have nonetheless borne them. On behalf of my people and my government, you see. But this once, just this once, I hoped to slip away incognito . . .

you do not recall the word? It means in secret, unannounced and unknown, remaining in a condition whereupon no one knows one's true identity . . . hence my early deception of you, you see." He spread his hands and smiled amiably. "In any event, I have had these past few weeks of freedom to draw upon. I shall remember them all the days of my life and think back to them with fondness and joy, these weeks when I have been able to pass among free men and women without obligation or restraint."

"Am I s'posed t' know what it is you're telling me, white man?"

"Please. Allow me to explain in my own good time and my own good manner. I do want it all to be clear to you, dear lady."

"That sure would be nice fo' a change, mistuh."

"Indeed." He graced her with his smile once again and this time patted her wrist gently. "I quite agree. My point, you see, is that once you bore the chains of bondage. I, my dear, have all my life borne the chains of obligation. As prince and heir to the throne of a sovereign nation. . . ."

"Say what?"

"As prince and heir is what I said, and prince and heir are what I am, I fear. Because of this accident of birth, Jeptha, I have never been able to move or act as a normal man might. Instead I have been obligated to say this and to wear that and never, ever to express an opinion other than the opinions of my father and his advisors."

"But—"

"Oh, I know what you are about to tell me, Jeptha. Have I not heard the same arguments all my life? Of course I have. And remember please that I myself admit that my chains are wrought of gold and gossamer. Poor little rich boy, that is what you are about to say. I cannot deny a word of it. I do not seek your sympathy for my plight. But I had, dear lady, hoped for your understanding. You see, this visit to the United States, unannounced and unheralded in your press, has been the only opportunity of my entire lifetime in which I could think and speak and move and act not as was expected of me but as I honestly and truly wished to do. On my own. Without prompting or counsel." He sighed hugely and now his smile was wan and distant as if in fond memory. "It was lovely while it lasted, Jeptha. But now, I suppose, I shall be forced to admit to my true identity. No doubt your government will make a fuss over my rescue from those brigands. Of course that will be all to the good so far as you and your tribe are concerned. The government no doubt will want to reward you lavishly for saving the life of a future leader of a friendly nation. Not with money, perhaps, so much as with food, horses, armaments. Did I mention the wonderfully talented armorers in my father's employ? Oh, such fine rifles they make. Marvelous devices, I'm told. I am sure my own government would be delighted to make a, um, substantial gift of that nature to you and your, uh, tribal companions. This in addition to whatever the United States government might choose to give to you, of course. That is only the right and proper thing for one to do. I will arrange it myself if need be. And I am glad for you and all your, um, friends here. Grateful to you and glad for you. Truly I am. My one regret is that now I must give up my own brief freedom and return to the limitations imposed upon me by circumstance. Once the United States government knows I am here, you understand. . . ." He shook his head sadly and lapsed into silence.

"You really a prince like you say?" Jeptha asked.

"You really got guns like you say?" a particularly unattractive young Indian warrior demanded. The man had been squatting only a few feet distant, to all intents and purposes fully absorbed in the examination of his own greasy hair braids. Now he spoke—in quite decent English—in deep and mellifluous tone.

J. Aubrey blinked.

"You got guns?" the Indian repeated.

"Not personally, no. My government, however, owns a factory which produces armaments for several of the standing armies on the Continent."

"Who you say?"

"Never mind. The point is, my government owns a factory that makes guns. Thousands of them. Tens of thousands. What of it?"

"You would give us guns?"

J. Aubrey shrugged. "I don't see why not," he said in all sincerity. He honestly knew of nothing to prevent it. Particularly when there was no truth in the offer and therefore there was nothing to actually prevent even if one wished to do so.

"Hairy-face damn blueleg soldiers don't want us to have guns," the Indian said. "Law says damn Injuns, we can't have guns."

J. Aubrey chuckled. "United States laws, perhaps. The laws in my country are different. Nothing against Indians having guns in my country. But then, you see, there would be no need for such a law even if one were deemed desirable. There are, ahem, no Indians in my country."

"What country that, huh?"

"Wales," J. Aubrey responded without pause. It was a question he had prepared in advance to answer. "Have you heard of it?"

The Indian shook his head.

"Wales is between England and Scotland. Do you know where those are?" In truth J. Aubrey was a trifle fuzzy himself on precisely where Wales lay. But he was sure it was in that neighborhood somewhere.

Again the Indian warrior shook his head.

"Pity," J. Aubrey said. "I was hoping you might know of it."

"Naw. No Injun there." The Indian grinned.

J. Aubrey laughed—perhaps more than the weak jest warranted—and slapped his thigh. "That was a good one, what?"

The Indian grinned again.

"Am I to understand, my good man, that the tribe would be, um, receptive to the gift of, say, several hundred new rifles?"

The Indian blinked and in rapid clucks and mutterings asked something of Jeptha, who responded in the same savage tongue.

"Bullet? Powder?" the Indian asked. He seemed quite excited now.

"Whatever," J. Aubrey said negligently. "I really don't know much about such things. Let's say two hundred rifles and whatever accoutrements should normally be issued with them, um?"

The Indian was so agitated now he seemed scarcely able to sit still. He reached over and tugged at the elbow of another warrior and tapped the thigh of a third, drawing their attention and they in turn expanding the circle.

Whispers were exchanged. And then louder voices.

The excitement filled the lodge and spilled outside. Within minutes there was a howling from around the big fire outdoors, the sound of it enough to chill a man to the marrow.

It occurred to J. Aubrey that it likely was a very good thing indeed that he would be long gone before these particular marks discovered the error of their faith in him.

He suspected that these lads would show remarkably little sense of charity toward anyone who gulled them.

But then what choice did he have, anyway? He certainly did not wish to contribute his scalp to one of the tripod displays that had sprung up in the camp during the day. Nor would he want to hang about and act indefinitely as a gatherer of buffalo chips.

No, the wise course, he was sure, would be to ask these Children of Nature to convey him into the protective custody of the nearest military establishment—what better way to discourage assault if premature discovery of the truth were to occur—and from there it would require no great talent to quietly disappear.

J. Aubrey smiled and sat back with contentment, secure in the knowledge that once again he had a future to plan toward. "I say, dear lady, didn't you tell me that you were the only person in the band who could speak English?" he asked idly.

Jeptha grinned and shrugged and said something back to him in the Indian language.

"Oh well," J. Aubrey told her. "You deceived me, but never fear. It is a favor I shan't choose to return. Aubrey, Prince of Wales, by the grace of God His Royal Highness, is never petty." And he tipped his head back and laughed with sheer, unfettered joy.

TWENTY-THREE

J. AUBREY SNIFFED. Loudly. And with disdain. The horse they mounted him upon was ancient and decrepit and barely able to support itself much less the added encumbrance of a rider. As a prince of the Welsh realm, J. Aubrey felt quite thoroughly insulted. On the other hand . . .

On the other hand, having any horse to ride—for that matter simply being alive and with an intact scalp—might be considered something of an improvement upon the situation he had undergone in the most recent past.

Still and all . . .

He sniffed again. Not quite so loudly this time. And thumped the elderly animal's ribs in an attempt to make the beast keep up with the others.

Not that the Indians were likely to allow him to wander off alone. They were candid to admit that this poor creature, possessing neither speed nor stamina, was chosen so that he could not reach civilized assistance without the connivance of his captors. That is to say, without the further help of his rescuers. He grunted. Semantics, it seemed, were as important to savage Lo as to the most sophisticated of gamesmen. Which J. Aubrey Whitford, Esq., most certainly considered himself to be.

Now the gentleman and sometime prince rode precariously atop this superannuated equine and did his best to do so with some modicum of dignity.

The Indian band had been traveling now for the better part of four days. Or what few remained in the group had been doing so. Most of the younger men, including the homely warrior who spoke English so remarkably well, had gone on ahead, disappearing the first morning soon after camp was broken. Since then J. Aubrey, in his role of princeling and benefactor, had been attended only by the women and the infirm and by a very small cadre of teenage warriors or would-be warriors. The grown men of fighting age had not been seen since it was agreed that the, um, guest should be conveyed to civilization by the swiftest possible means. The understanding, of course, was that the Prince of Wales would be placed into the protective care of the United States military and that the Indian band would be recompensed and rewarded by a grateful Welsh government. And perhaps by the government of the United States of America as well. Prince Aubrey had been understandably reluctant to make pledges against the budget of any nation other than his own. The Indians had been commendably understanding about that.

But all of that had been decided days and days ago. By now J. Aubrey, which is to say Prince Aubrey of the House of Whitford, heir to the throne of Wales, was quite heartily weary of constant travel and bad food.

At least, he consoled himself, he was no longer required to gather chips for the nightly cooking fires. The women— that swollen-headed, uppity Jeptha among them—were made to do all of that.

He sniffed again, partially mollified by the fact that Jeptha was required to work and he was not. That was something.

And he was assured, repeatedly, that the military encampment they sought was only a little ways farther on. Just a little distance more and this most unpleasant interruption would be done with. He would be free once more to pursue his heart; free once more to pursue Miss Grace in all her purity and promise.

J. Aubrey sought to maintain his balance atop the bony mount that he straddled and sought at the same time to look ahead to that stellar moment when he would catch up to Miss Grace and once again be able to take her into his arms, to press his lips to her lovely cheek, to feel her slender form close against . . .

The damnable horse stumbled and nearly spilled him from the cloth padding that was all the Indians allowed him for a saddle. J. Aubrey yelped and teetered but did not topple. He was, just this once, not unhappy about the interruption of his thoughts. Some things, after all, are simply too painful to bear.

TWENTY-FOUR

"THERE." Jeptha rose in her stirrups and pointed. "See there?"

J. Aubrey stared in the direction indicated, but all he could see was a distant tree line that was a low green smudge between the drab brown uniformity that was the prairie and the pale blue-white emptiness that was the sky. If there was any one statement that could be made about this western country without fear of error or contradiction it was that the land here was a perfect model of monotony.

"You don't see that, white man?"

"What I see is . . . ," he frowned, "never mind what I see. The point is, I don't see anything worth looking at."

"There," the Negress insisted, jabbing at the air quite forcefully in that same direction over and over again. "You see that thing flutter like bird flying in one place? Right there?"

Reluctantly J. Aubrey shrugged. Perhaps he saw what she meant. But what of it. He'd seen birds before this.

"So'jer flag there, white man. We reach them trees, you be big prince again. Give guns like you promise. Ha. Them damn so'jer gonna be mad to you, white man. But you promise, yes? You give guns like you say."

"I did promise," J. Aubrey affirmed in a sonorously serious tone. "I shall so comply, my dear woman, regardless of the wishes of the government of your, um, United States." His choice of voice was deliberately low and resonant. But then he was, as it were, practicing. Because it was one thing to fool a bunch of illiterate savages. It would be quite another to carry off the deception in front of a group of professional military men of the officer class. And he judged it would be wise to at least try to carry the game through long enough for the Indians to depart this place still of the impression that their reward would someday be paid. After all, J. Aubrey had no desire for the rascals to loiter in wait for him should they discover the truth too early.

Still and all, despite the many mental and emotional preparations he had to make as they approached the now perfectly visible army encampment—and those preparations can scarcely be appreciated by anyone who has never undertaken to convincingly assume a gamesman's role, since one must not merely act the charade, one must *be* it clear through to the core—he could not help a concomitant stirring of excitement as the band of horsemen wended nearer and nearer to the village of white tents that marked the military outpost.

As the horses plodded close even the Indians sat up straighter and began to exhibit an eagerness of anticipation.

But then they were expecting gifts and feasting and whatever else it was that accompanied these meetings of two diverse cultures on the barren plains. J. Aubrey understood that because of the translations provided to him by the woman Jeptha.

For the past day and a half the moving Indian band had been visited by couriers from the body of warriors. Apparently those hardy souls had ridden swiftly ahead and were already in communication with the soldiers. Riders shuttled back and forth between that group and the oncoming band of elders and women who served as protectors and companions to the, uh, guest of honor, His Royal Highness J. Aubrey.

Jeptha did not explain in detail, but J. Aubrey gathered that certain negotiations were undertaken and agreements reached. Even though he understood this fully, he hastened to assure the elders that he intended to honor his own commitments to the group. The arms and accoutrements would be delivered as promised, separate and apart from any agreement the band might make with the soldiers. And apart, as well, from any objection or blockade that might be raised by those same soldiers.

"If I must," the prince explained patiently on more than one occasion, "I shall have His Excellency my father transport your armaments by way of Canada." And at that point in his discourse he never failed to remind these unsophisticates that "no member of the House of Whitford has ever broken faith with his fellows nor abandoned his solemn word of honor, never in all recorded history; of that you can be sure; of that you have my holy word." At which time, Lo being fearsome and bloodthirsty but in many ways childlike and innocent, J. Aubrey always went through a ritual that was meant to impress by way of its pageantry. The ritual, which he had come to think of as The Prince's Pledge, consisted of kneeling, crossing oneself, kissing the knuckle of the right thumb, using that thumb in a gesture suggestive of self-disembowelment, kissing the knuckle of the left thumb, slicing that thumb backward across the throat as if again to suggest Death Before Dishonor, crossing himself a second time and finally extending a fisted hand palm downward in the direction of the Indian headman. It was all a lot of hooey, of course. But the Indians appeared to be impressed by the prince's homemade ritual. And what more could a gentleman ask than that.

J. Aubrey did not attempt to explain what any of it purported to mean. And curious though he was, he knew better than to ask what interpretation the savages might place upon all or any of his theatrics.

All of that was behind him now, of course. Now he sat up as straight as he dared on the swaybacked nag that bore him closer and ever closer to safety.

Now rescue, the true version and not an ersatz imitation as when the Indians "rescued" him from the Bokampers, was within hailing distance.

Now he could see soldiers in blue uniforms standing staunch on parade before the flagpole, blue-coated soldiers with rifles and bayonets and white canvas strapping criss-crossing their torsos, standing proud and erect beneath the flapping, snapping, fluttering Bright Stars and Broad Stripes. Oh, it was a grand and a glorious sight, and if he hadn't been a prince from Wales, why, J. Aubrey might well have burst into patriotic song.

As it was, he contented himself with puffing his chest in shared pride with these fine young men whose appearance was in such sharp contrast with the slovenly, grease-streaked countenances of the savage visitors with whom J. Aubrey rode.

"Comp'ny," a voice bawled in wonderful, welcome English, "ten-SHUN."

Shoe heels clapped solidly together, and dust rose from the earth at the base of the line of crisply attentive soldiers.

"Pree-zent . . . HARMS."

A sword flashed silver in the sunlight, and a score or more of rifles were lifted and smartly slapped as if by a single hand.

From somewhere off to the side a drum flourish rattled and fifes began to play.

An officer whose chin seemed to be stuck tight against his own Adam's apple came pigeon-walking forward with an unnatural, stiff-legged gait, his chest out and gut in and ears red from exertion. "Sir," he bellowed loud enough to be heard by anyone within half a mile. "Welcome to the United States of America. Sir. I mean . . . Your Excellency. Sir." The officer's ears grew redder yet.

J. Aubrey puffed his own chest just a little. Well now. Yes indeed now. Goodness gracious, yes. The Indians really had been laying it on thick, mmm?

After an introduction like this, why, it would be criminal to let all that groundwork be wasted.

J. Aubrey Whitford, that is to say His Royal Highness Aubrey of the House of Whitford, cleared his throat with a harrumph or two and sat for a moment surveying these subjects. Then, as if giving a benediction, he raised a languid hand and sniffed. "Theng-kew," he mumbled as if quite, quite bored with this whole silly procedure. "Have you my quarters ready? My bath? My cook? Um?" He withdrew the hand that had been lifted in greeting and now turned it about so as to examine his fingernails. His expression was accusing, as if any dirt he might find under those nails was the direct responsibility of this officer and these troops and they really *better* do better by him in future, what?

"At once, Your Excellency. We'll see to all of that at once, sir, I promise."

His Royal Highness only sniffed. And sat with his chin held high while he waited to be helped down from the dreadful horse.

He hadn't long to wait.

TWENTY-FIVE

A BATH. Good heavens, there was an actual tub available at this rustic outpost. J. Aubrey had mentioned the word "bath." The commander of the post, a red-haired and befreckled caricature of an army captain named Dinwittie—and mustn't his childhood have been an adventure in barbed comment—pounced upon the distinguished visitor's whim as if it were command and promptly sent the enlisted men into a flurry of activity that was intended to bring succor and comfort to His Royal Highness.

J. Aubrey slid lower into the tub, a clever object of waterproofed canvas suspended within a framework of bright ash, until his shoulders were submerged and the bottoms of his earlobes brushed teasingly against the layer of suds that floated upon the lukewarm water. He could not remember being so comfortable in ever so long now. In fact, he was not at all sure that he had ever before been quite this comfortable, the difference between this and all previous occasions being a matter of appreciation. On this particular occasion J. Aubrey Whitford well understood the pleasure of remaining alive. All else built from that most enjoyable base.

He sighed, wriggled, burrowed deep within the warm cocoon of bathwater. He yawned and let his head loll back with his eyes closed. This, surely, was what Heaven must be like. This most certainly was a foretaste of a benevolent Hereafter.

One hand broke the surface of the water and snaked out beyond the layer of suds, blindly seeking the stool that had been so conveniently positioned beside the tub to serve as a side table. Eyes still closed, J. Aubrey located the glass and brought the sharply aromatic brandy to his lips. Captain Dinwittie's tipple smelled wonderful and tasted even better. J. Aubrey smiled and tossed off this third or fourth—no one was counting—and enjoyed the ensuing sensation of warmth that infused his belly.

"Well, ain't you got it made," a grating voice snarled from somewhere nearby. J. Aubrey opened his eyes.

The man who had spoken was, not surprisingly, a soldier. A lowly private, J. Aubrey judged. Not that he had any expertise in that area, but the soldier's state of slovenly dress and lack of adornment on his jacket would seem to indicate a person of the lowest possible rank in the mostly incomprehensible military scheme of things. The fellow was thin and dark and long of face. He stood off to one side with an armload of fresh towels and no place to put them.

"On the cot there will be fine, my good man," J. Aubrey suggested. "And, um, were you addressing me?"

The soldier snorted. Derisively. Unkindly. And rather loudly.

"What was that again?" J. Aubrey asked.

"You, mister. You got it made. Leastways you think you do. But I know sum'pin that you don't."

"And what might that be?" J. Aubrey asked quite pleasantly.

"I be knowin' about the real Prince o' Wales, mister. Which ain't you."

J. Aubrey gave the cheeky rascal a haughty stare. The damnable soldier did not back off so much as a mite. Worse, after a few moments the soldier began to grin. And then to laugh outright.

"Hell," the fellow drawled, the sound of it coming out more like "hail," "I gotta give you credit. You got these popinjays a-poppin'. So y' do, mister." He glanced around and spotted the aforementioned cot which was the only available piece of furniture in the tent that served as quarters for the most distinguished visitor His Royal Highness J. Aubrey Whitford. The soldier plopped his armful of towels on one end of the cot and himself on the other. With a chuckle he helped himself to a cigar from the full box that had been provided by Captain Dinwittie.

"Would you care for a cigar?" J. Aubrey intoned some moments after the fact.

"Thanks, mister. Don't mind if I do." He trimmed and lighted the smoke, then left his seat on J. Aubrey's bed long enough to come over and help himself to a slug of brandy, drinking it straight from the flask.

"And perhaps a dram as well," J. Aubrey said rather dryly.

"No, thanks. I never drink."

"As you wish."

The man returned to his perch on the cot, crossed his legs and sat there for a time happily puffing on the cigar.

"Now what is this nonsense about, um . . . ?"

"The Prince o' Wales?" The man grinned. Came over and had another pull at the brandy flask. Went back to the cot and grinned some more. "Mister, you got a nice idea goin' here. But you picked the wrong title. That's all you done wrong, mind. Just that title. Lucky for you that Dinwittie is a dim-witty, and that's the moral truth."

"See here now . . . ," J. Aubrey commenced, quite prepared to puff up and bluster if need be.

"Now, don't you be gettin' yourself in a uproar. No need for that. Hail, man, I admire your nerve. I do."

J. Aubrey gave the cheeky fellow a look calculated to wither.

The soldier failed even to wilt.

Instead he grinned.

"The Prince o' Wales, m' man, is named Edward. An' he's eleven years of age. Which means, mister, that *you* ain't *him.*"

The soldier had a look now like a cat with bright yellow canary feathers wreathing its mouth. He helped himself to yet another tot of J. Aubrey's fine brandy and puffed smugly on the cigar.

There really was a Prince of Wales? Whoever would have thought it. J. Aubrey sank a trifle lower into his bathwater and pretended a lack of concern. But . . . there really *was* a Prince of Wales? Drat.

TWENTY-SIX

J. AUBREY STOOD with his chin held high and his fine, leonine head posed as if offering an image suitable for striking upon commemorative coinage. He cut a handsome figure now that he was bathed and dressed in new linen donated to him by the officers of the regiment, battalion, whatever. He puffed the swatch of delicate foulard tied at his throat, shot his cuffs, harrumphed twice to clear his throat.

Night had fallen whilst he bathed, and now there was to be a celebration in his honor. The gala occasion commingled red men and white together, the male Indians who were J. Aubrey's recent captors ranged in semicircle round about a hugely flaring bonfire while the remainder of the arc was filled in by officers and higher-ranking noncoms squatting in cross-legged imitation of their savage visitors. Leaping flames and moving figures created a wild and almost frightening background of bright light and deep shadow that twined and twisted without pattern.

J. Aubrey held his thoroughly calculated pose until his arrival was noted. He hadn't long to wait.

"All rise. All rise, please," Captain Dinwittie yelped, his voice starting out deep and authoritative enough but soon breaking into a shrill squeak. The post commander set an example for the others to follow by leaping frantically to his feet and rushing to greet this awesomely distinguished guest.

The other officers came to their feet, as did the enlisted men who had been allowed the honor of attendance. The whites clicked to rigid attention. The Indians retained their seats and reached for the bowls and platters of food that had been placed on blankets.

"On your feet. You there, up, everyone up," Dinwittie urged of the Indians. One of the savages—the homely rascal who belatedly acknowledged acquaintance with the English language—muttered something that was much too low for J. Aubrey to overhear. Whatever it was, Captain Dinwittie flushed a bright, beety shade. The Indian helped himself to a platter of steaming hot corn dodgers, drawing the crockery platter into his lap and balancing it there. He seemed much more interested in munching than in manners.

Captain Dinwittie had no more time to spend upon the cheeky Indian. Instead the officer scurried to J. Aubrey's side, took a moment to compose himself while standing at attention and then abruptly nodded.

J. Aubrey jumped, startled by the blare of unexpected noise that pierced the night from somewhere left of the ring of firelight.

It took him a moment to realize that the racket was deliberate and almost, if not quite, melodic. A post band, of sorts, had been assembled in honor of the occasion. There were bugles and drums. He was sure of those. And perhaps several less readily identifiable instruments as well. The noise they made might have been tolerable had all of them been performing the same tune, he suspected. He smiled benignly and graciously consented to nod in the direction of the band. Rather reluctantly he stopped short of lifting a hand in silent benediction. He wasn't entirely clear, after all, on the subject of behavior appropriate to his status. Particularly in view of the information recently gained. So he settled for benevolence in the stead of benediction.

"If you would care to come this way, Your Royal Highness," Dinwittie intoned, bowing.

"A moment, my good fellow."

"Sir?"

"There is a matter I should mention to you, um, before we

join the savages. Some of whom understand English quite well even if they do not own up to the accomplishment."

"But—"

"Hear me out, Captain."

"As you wish, Your Highness." The fellow bowed again, his subservience bringing a certain warmth of good will and happiness into J. Aubrey's chest.

"You should understand, Captain, that I am not precisely as I seem."

"Sir?"

"The truth is that I am not actually entitled to be called Royal Highness."

"But—"

"I am not the Prince of Wales, Captain."

"But. . . ." Less confusion this time. A scowl seemed imminent.

"Shush, Captain. You forget yourself. I am, you understand, in the line of succession. But only if the real Prince of Wales were to expire. I used the grander title in hope of impressing those rude creatures over there who are bent upon eating you out of house and home at one seating. My actual title, you see, is earl. I am Aubrey, Earl of Whitford, second cousin to His Royal Highness Edward, Prince of Wales."

Dinwittie blinked.

"You should understand, Captain, that I am entitled to be called Your Excellency. That is to say, My Excellency. That is to say, you should refer to me as 'Your Excellency.' But not by the more distinguished appellation, Your Royal Highness. Not until or unless young Edward expires, at which time I would of course be more directly in line for the throne. The throne, I might add, not only of Wales but of England also."

Dinwittie acted as if he'd been jabbed with a particularly sharp pin. He gasped.

"I did not want to mention that to the Indians, you understand, because it would only confuse them. I assume they know about the queen, beloved grandmother of the Indian tribes in far northern Canada." He had read that somewhere. Or had he only imagined it? No matter. True or not it would serve to confuse poor Dinwittie, a task that was easily accomplished. "What I suggest you do, Captain, is continue my charade until the savages have received their gifts and taken leave of this site. Then, of course, I shall revert to my true status as earl but not prince. From the point of view of your government, however, I suspect the difference would be deemed slight. The fact remains that I am part of the royal succession."

"But—"

"Don't interrupt me, my dear fellow. That simply isn't done." J. Aubrey braced Dinwittie with a tightening of his lips that only approximated a smile.

"I beg your pardon, sir." Dinwittie bowed again.

"Sire."

"Sir?"

"I was correcting you. 'Sire' is more appropriate to my rank than your 'sir' would be."

"Oh. Yes. Um, sire."

This time J. Aubrey's expression was a smile. Thin. But a smile nonetheless. Captain Dinwittie seemed grateful for the amelioration.

"But you should refer to me as My, Your, as Royal Highness only while the savages remain. Once they are away you may address me as Your Excellency."

"Of course. Sire." The man's lips quivered in anticipation of his reward. He received it. In the form this time of a much broader and brighter smile from Aubrey, Earl of Whitford. "Shall we, um, join the festivities now, sire?"

"Yes, in one more moment."

"There was something else, sire?"

"One thing only. My chapeau. I wish for it to be recovered from the dastard who purloined it."

"Sire?"

"My hat, man. My beaver hat. That greasy Indian over there is wearing my hat. I want it back. Forthwith. If he objects, tell him there will be no guns paid over for my release."

"Guns, sire?"

"Dear me, you are in the dark about things, aren't you, Captain."

"I'm afraid so, sire."

"It isn't important, really. Just that the Indians are expecting armaments. Don't look at me like that. I had to promise them something, didn't I? I shan't deliver any weapons to them, of course. Couldn't, you see. Earls do not command armies as princes might, you understand. But the savages needn't know that. Just let them wander off thinking the reward will be brought to them eventually. They'll not know otherwise for years, and by that time they will likely have forgotten all about it anyway."

Dinwittie, for some reason, seemed quite perfectly appalled. "But sire . . . these Indians . . . they have long memories. And a great regard for the truth."

J. Aubrey smiled. Benignly. "All the better then. It is the honest man who is the most gullible."

The army captain frowned. "I don't think you understand the consequences a broken promise can have with these people."

Aubrey, Earl of Whitford, sniffed haughtily. "You forget yourself, Captain. Or must I discuss this uncooperative attitude with your superiors?"

"As you wish, sire," the now quite miserable and trembling officer sniveled.

J. Aubrey sniffed again, squared his shoulders and began striding boldly into the circle of firelight.

Over his shoulder he gave Dinwittie a stern reminder. "My hat, man. Don't forget my hat."

This time the obsequious little red-haired captain failed to respond, and J. Aubrey sailed onward with regal mien, taking his place as the guest of honor and center of attention, both seeming very much his due after the many travails so recently weathered.

But all of that was behind him now.

Now he could once again get about the serious business of seeking out his one, his own, his great and true love Miss Grace.

Just as soon as these stupid Indians were mollified and sent safely away.

Really it was quite all he could manage to keep from offering a benediction over the assemblage that had gathered to honor him.

Instead Aubrey, Earl of Whitford, smiled and smiled and smiled.

TWENTY-SEVEN

J. AUBREY SNIFFED. *Most* useful, the supercilious sniff. As he was rapidly learning. It expressed disdain for a multitude of offenses, conveyed superiority and turned aside much of the necessity for comment—all in a single, marvelously versatile gesture.

And of those the most valuable was without doubt the elimination of need for comment. Because discussion, J. Aubrey was learning, could be quite dangerous.

There was simply so very much he did not know about the business of being noble.

Noble by birth and blood, that is.

J. Aubrey Whitford, with or without the guise of royal lineage, considered himself most noble indeed. Because true nobility, J. Aubrey Whitford's form of nobility, resided neither in surname nor nomenclature but in force of character, in a nobility of the spirit, in one's own unflagging belief in self-worth.

That, J. Aubrey believed, was the truest nobility of them all.

As for this other—he smiled a bit but in silence, directing it inward—as for this other he would milk it for every jot or tittle.

He sniffed again, not quite so loudly this time, and with languid gesture turned a wrist so as to examine his recently cleaned and shortened fingernails. "You begin to bore me," he droned as if to himself.

"But Your Excellency . . . sire. . . ."

"Must I repeat myself, Captain?"

"No, I suppose not." The man sounded quite satisfyingly defeated.

"No *what,* Dinwittie?"

"No, *sire.* Your Excellency. Your . . ." He stammered to a halt before anything more might trickle out.

Temper, temper, J. Aubrey silently chided, carefully hiding his own amusement at the military wretch's misery.

But then the poor fellow's royal visitor *was* being a royal pain.

J. Aubrey—that is to say, Aubrey, Earl of Whitford—plucked a silken handkerchief from his cuff and delicately coughed into it. He feigned a yawn. "What was it you were saying, Dinwittie?"

"I was, um, saying, sire, that, uh, I will take personal charge of the escort force and, um, give you my personal guarantees—"

"The numbers, Dinwittie, the numbers. How many men are you giving me?"

"But sire, surely you understand that I simply cannot devote my entire force to your escort. There are others who need protection along the trade routes every bit as much as you might. . . ."

J. Aubrey sniffed again. Loudly this time. Dinwittie moaned slightly. Wilted even more.

J. Aubrey was certain that soon the man would break completely and agree, despite his best judgment on the matter, that the Earl of Whitford be escorted to safety by no less than the entire available force now posted in this incredibly insignificant little backwater.

J. Aubrey was demanding precisely that. And so far Dinwittie had been foolishly resisting compliance with the Earl of Whitford's demands. Never mind what the fellow's orders or his mission might be.

The thing was, J. Aubrey—not the Earl but the real J. Aubrey Whitford—was living in a state of near terror and would continue to do so until he once again was free of these awful plains and safely ensconced within the protective bounds of civilization.

Because while the savages might be gone from this encampment, they were close indeed to J. Aubrey's thoughts.

In fact, they might reasonably be said to have invested his thoughts so thoroughly, and so frighteningly, that he had little capacity for thought on any other subject.

He shuddered again now just from thinking about that. The memory was perfectly horrid; the actual event had been even worse.

It had been—he couldn't forget it, couldn't block it from his mind no matter how hard he tried—it had been in the small hours of the night. Long after the Indians ceremoniously took the gifts the army gave them, gifts of food and gifts of merchandise, things like mirrors and beads and unsharpened bits of flat steel shaped and ready to be formed into knives, and mounted their ponies whilst wearing their best and most fancy finery and rode away, all of them rode away, J. Aubrey himself had *seen* them all ride away. He shuddered again.

He had with his own eyes seen the Indians depart. He went so far as to count them as their procession formed into single file on the open area that the soldiers regarded as a parade ground. All of the savages were accounted for. The headman and the woman Jeptha and most particularly of all that hideously ugly individual who spoke English. They left. All of them. Without exception.

And that had been in the forenoon of the day in question so that surely by nightfall the band should have been, would have been, many, many miles distant. Out of sight, out of reach, out of J. Aubrey's thoughts and concerns forever and ever more.

Except—the breath caught in his throat—except that night, that very *night,* he was awakened in his bed.

Awakened by the unwelcome sensation of having a hard hand clapped roughly over his mouth. Awakened by the stench of rancid grease and woodsmoke and other vile odors it perhaps was best not to identify. Awakened in his own bed despite the fact that a guard was posted as a courtesy and could even at that moment be heard to march back and forth outside the tent where Aubrey, Earl of Whitford, slept.

Awakened by that damnable English-speaking Indian.

"You. White man." J. Aubrey even now could hear the words ringing within his thoughts and exacerbating his fears. "You do not forget your promise. Because we do not forget. You bring guns like you promise, white man. Or we find you. Take your scalp to hang on my drum, white man. Take scalp before you die, eh? Take scalp first and then kill you." There was a sound, a dimly heard howl from the pits of Hell itself, that pretended to be laughter. And then, the most menacing words of all, the Indian said, "Kill you if you lucky, white man." And that awful laugh again.

And then the Indian was gone without a whisper of sound.

One moment he was there. The next he was not.

And still the soldier with the musket and bayonet marched slowly back and forth a few paces distant.

J. Aubrey had not slept a moment since. Nor did he expect to for however long he remained in this awful place.

J. Aubrey lifted his nose higher into the air and peered down the length of it at meek and miserable Dinwittie.

"All of them, Your Excellency. The escort will be conducted by my entire force, sire, as you wish."

"Quickly," J. Aubrey added to his list of demands, not deigning to acknowledge his victory on the size of the escort. But then of course the victory was no more than was his due as earl and heir. Whyever should he bother to comment upon it? "I wish to leave here as quickly as possible."

"Of course, sire. Whatever you desire, Your Excellency."

J. Aubrey dabbed a soft fold of silk at his left nostril and then at the right. "Better, Dinwittie. Much better."

"Thank you, Your Excellency."

Aubrey, Earl of Whitford, sniffed.

TWENTY-EIGHT

HOW VERY ODD. And odder still that he hadn't thought of it beforehand. The truth, though, was that Aubrey, Earl of Whitford, was entirely unprepared for the hullabaloo that greeted his arrival in the settlement—it could hardly be considered a town, being even smaller and less prepossessing than Esmeraldaville, Texas—known as Cowpen's Lick in the unassigned lands that were coming to be known informally as Kansas. Cowpen's Lick. The very name was enough to make a gentleman's nose wrinkle. The implications were of livestock and gamy creatures and other such disgusting things.

Still, what could anyone expect of the residents of such a burg when they were honored with a visit from the nobility?

The aspect J. Aubrey had failed to consider was that these buffoons might have received advance notice of the impending visitation. Obviously, somehow, they had been forewarned.

When the column of marching infantry limped sweating into the confines of Cowpen's Lick with Aubrey, Earl of Whitford, riding in an ambulance at their head—both column and ambulance unmolested by savages since leaving the distant army post, by the bye—they were greeted by banners and bunting, everything a patriotic red, white and blue and presumably left over from July Fourth celebrations, and greeted by a populace numbering considerably more than J. Aubrey would have believed could live in so small a community. In the event, it transpired that his assumptions were correct on that subject. People had gathered for many,

many miles around in order to assemble at Cowpen's Lick in such quantity.

As a good American, J. Aubrey was touched.

As Aubrey, Earl of Whitford, he was somewhat less impressed with the display.

He sniffed.

Loudly.

"What's wrong now, Your Excellency?" Dinwittie, who had been required to walk beside His Excellency's makeshift coach ever since leaving the army post some days past —one could not permit an underling to ride horseback and thereby place himself at a height superior to that of the earl, could one?—asked, sounding soul-weary as well as physically fatigued. J. Aubrey was beginning to suspect that Captain Dinwittie would consider himself fortunate to take final leave of his country's noble guest.

"Those colorful displays, man. Are they deliberately insulting? Or is that a logical extension of the stupidity of the citizenry here?"

"I beg your pardon, sire?"

"Am I mistaken, Captain, or do those color combinations signify an insult to the queen? I shouldn't want to have to report to Her Majesty that she is held in light regard here, y'know. Not when your nation's leaders in Washington are in the process of begging financial assistance from Her Majesty yet again." About which J. Aubrey had no knowledge whatsoever save a generalized understanding that nations incessantly beg from one another; any statement to that effect could be made with scant fear of error.

Dinwittie, his eyes a trifle glassy, mumbled apologies that he pretended to mean and which J. Aubrey in turn pretended to accept.

Aubrey, Earl of Whitford, sniffed again. But only lightly this time. Dinwittie affected not to have heard.

The ambulance rolled to a halt adjacent to a reviewing stand that was surrounded by shabbily dressed men who had the appearance of being farmers and common laborers and the like. On the decorated stand a much better dressed and more prosperous delegation was waiting to greet the distinguished visitor from distant climes.

"Your Royal Highness," one of them began. Loudly. A young lieutenant broke away from the column of soldiers and dashed to the side of the viewing platform in time to tug at the coattails of the introductory speaker. The speaker, a large man with beefy jowls and a belly to match, scowled at the interruption but gave in to the importunate officer and leaned down for a moment. The lieutenant whispered hurried warnings, and the large man resumed his orator's stance and once more cleared his throat. "Your, um, Excellency . . . welcome to Cowpen's Lick." He seemed put off a bit by the last-moment correction. But as any good statesman should be able, he recovered quickly and was soon engaged in a soaring commentary that touched briefly on relations between Britain and the United States of America —J. Aubrey found it interesting that the fellow managed to accomplish this without ever once mentioning any past disagreements between these sister-like nations—and democracy in general and the salubrious business climate of the Great American West and many, many other subjects, to which J. Aubrey paid no particular attention. As Aubrey, Earl of Whitford, he sat and pretended to listen while he scanned the crowd in hope of seeing Miss Grace among those assembled. A crowd like this should be an irresistible attraction for any scammer. Miss Grace should have been drawn to it as surely as a moth is drawn to flame. Yet try as he might he could catch no glimpse of her. He had to content himself with allowing the drone of the speaker's voice to fill his ears while he surveyed the crowd a second time, seeking this time not his own dear Miss Grace but any rounded cheek or lowered eyelash pretty enough to ease the pangs of boredom and encourage innocent flights of fancy.

Sadly, however, he was forced to conclude that the farmers of this country, so backward that it was neither state nor even administered territory, were given to marriage with women suitable for service in the fields as scarecrows.

The few women within eyesight of the ambulance where Aubrey, Earl of Whitford, so patiently waited had flesh so spare and desiccated as to remind him of a mummified monkey he had seen on display once in a museum near the wharfs in dear New York, New York.

And why oh *why* had he made the mistake now of thinking about home? Such home as he had, that is. A home of inclination if not of fact.

This time Aubrey, Earl of Whitford, did not sniff. This time he sighed. Sadly.

Here he was. Infinitely far from both the one person in all the world he held dear and the one place as well.

He might have wept. Except that would not be seemly in an earl of the realm.

Instead he could only sit, disconsolate, while the speaker droned on through most of the remaining daylight . . . and it had been barely past noon when the column of soldiers, still standing in close formation, reached Cowpen's Lick.

TWENTY-NINE

THE EARL OF WHITFORD pursed his lips and, with a most sour expression, sloshed the liquid from cheek to cheek as if rinsing his mouth. He cast his eyes wildly about and groped blindly for the water tumbler that belonged to his neighbor at the table, a Miss Wiscowicz. The lady blinked in alarm and, perceiving the intentions of her guest, held the tumbler to his lips so that he could spit out the offending substance. "Your Excellency, is there something wro—"

J. Aubrey grunted and, his expression still sour, complained, "Wrong? Is that what you ask? You serve me something like this and then ask if there is something wrong? Really, madame. Really!"

The woman blanched a pale and pasty white and gaped across the table at her brother, the community's most prosperous entrepreneur and leading citizen, he of lengthy speeches and strong body odor, Buford Wiscowicz. "Bufe," the lady whined in a shrill and unlovely tone. "You tole me that was s'posed to be the best, Bufe. Now His Excellency don' like it, Bufe. Why don' you like that wine, Your Excellency?" Neither tone nor volume altered when the woman shifted her focus of attention from brother to guest.

Aubrey, Earl of Whitford, sniffed and again made a face. "That, madame, was no wine. It barely qualifies as a vinegar. A disreputable vinegar at that, I say." He rolled his eyes and looked away. Quickly lest he break into laughter and ruin the whole thing.

Edna Mae Wiscowicz reeled back to slump, aghast, against the padded back of her chair. She appeared a woman well on her way to swooning.

The man sitting to her right, a merchant named Dockery, waved his napkin in her face to provide more air and forestall the impending faint. Buford Wiscowicz leaped from his chair and raced around to lend a supporting arm to his sagging sister. "But . . . but . . . but . . ." In his state of agitation Buford grabbed the water tumbler and held it to his sister's lips so she could drink and calm herself. Neither of them noticed that the water was tainted with wine. Which J. Aubrey had just expectorated into the vessel.

Aubrey, Earl of Whitford, sniffed again and said, "No matter. I shall take tea instead of claret, mm?"

Wiscowicz snapped his fingers and in the shadows there was a scuffle of scurrying feet as servants raced to obey. Edna Mae opened her eyes and was able to breathe more deeply now that the crisis had passed and His Excellency was clearly remaining at the table. J. Aubrey suspected, however, that Edna Mae would instruct ol' Bufe about his lack of taste ere this night was ended. Whether or not Buford suffered from such a lack. The truth was that one wine tasted much like any other so far as J. Aubrey Whitford was concerned. The claret he'd rejected could very well have been the finest in the land and he would never know the difference. He'd only voiced objection on a whim.

That little flurry was the most fun J. Aubrey had had since the Wiscowiczes commandeered him from Captain Dinwittie as their prize house guest.

No doubt this visit from an authentic—insofar as anyone in Cowpen's Lick knew, anyway—earl would be the focus of conversation and the apex of social achievement hereabouts for—who knew—perhaps for hundreds of miles and through decades to come. Certainly the Wiscowiczes would never forget it.

J. Aubrey only hoped that unlike his hosts, who would remember him forever, he might be blessed with complete forgetfulness concerning them. And as quickly as possible at that. Buford and Edna Mae Wiscowicz were not among his very most favorite people. There was something about them. . . .

Still, even as the Earl of Whitford he could be only so selective. After all, he was more or less obligated to put up only with the very best. And when it came to this dreary parcel of nowhere, Buford and Edna Mae apparently were as good as it got.

Which said rather a great deal about the populace here.

Buford Wiscowicz was a portly, puffy individual of middle years with lank, thinning hair and a disposition that said he was accustomed to being in charge. His only slightly younger spinster sister Edna Mae was a massive, bovine creature who would have benefited from instruction in the proper application of hair dyes. Whatever concoction she now used fell considerably short of success, the result having an appearance much like that of straw basketwork that had been immersed in boot black. J. Aubrey might have considered offering the poor woman some of his own ink— it could have done no worse a job of it—but as the Earl of Whitford was quite naturally unable to do so.

Apart from the Wiscowiczes, in whose mansion the earl was to reside whilst in Cowpen's Lick, the dinner guests assembled at the long table included Dockery and his young wife Sue—rather fetching young wife Sue, J. Aubrey would have noticed, although the Earl of Whitford took no note of that whatsoever—and eight other couples placed in boy-girl, boy-girl arrangement down both sides of the table, making for a total seating of twenty-one. No doubt it rankled Edna Mae that an odd number of guests were seated, but then that could hardly be helped. Even Edna Mae Wiscowicz would not have been boorish enough to suggest selecting a female companion for the Earl of Whitford, not from among the ladies available in this backwater.

Once past Dockery and his wife, J. Aubrey's memory for the names of his dining companions diminished. There was the fellow whose name was James. But J. Aubrey could no longer recall if that was his first name or his last. And there was a woman named Letitia. A man called Paul. Too many to bother trying to remember, anyway.

Perhaps significantly, there were no military personnel at the table, either because the Wiscowiczes chose to snub such government employees or, more likely, because Dinwittie and his men wanted shut of the Earl of Whitford at the earliest possible opportunity. Not that J. Aubrey minded. He was just as happy having been turned over to civilian authority for the time being.

In addition to the score-plus-one of diners, the table was surrounded by dark-skinned servants who labored to present an impression of elegance where none existed.

At the moment they were busy taking bottles of the offensive claret away and replacing them on the linen with cups and saucers. And when those ran out with mugs instead, such proletarian items being relegated to the far lower reaches of the table.

J. Aubrey was finding the whole process amusing.

A servant came near and squatted at Buford's side. "Shall I serve now, suh?"

"Yes, I suppose so, I . . ." The host's voice choked off, and he stared in the direction of the far end of the room. He seemed quite startled.

Swiftly other eyes noticed, swiveled, peered all together in that same direction.

J. Aubrey could do no less.

He gasped.

Almost as one, every man in the room came to his feet. And Aubrey, Earl of Whitford, did the same, leaping into motion before he had time to give thought to whether this was appropriate for an earl's behavior.

Nor would he have done differently had he taken time to research the question in exhaustive detail.

He simply could not have remained seated. Not and thought of himself as being any sort of gentleman.

Not when the most beautiful young woman he had ever in his life espied was at that very moment standing within the entryway to the Wiscowicz dining hall.

THIRTY

THE YOUNG WOMAN—girl—appeared to be seventeen or within a year of it, one direction or the other. Which is to say nubile. But only just.

Despite the strong sense of devotion J. Aubrey felt toward Miss Grace, he nonetheless could not fail to respond to the beauty of this maiden.

His breath came quick in his breast and he found himself braced to his most upright and statuesque pose, jaw lifted impressively and head turned the least bit so as to be presented to the lady at the most favorable angle of view. Even without the trappings of titled nobility, J. Aubrey Whitford cut a fine figure. No immodesty attached to recognition of the obvious, and the years had taught J. Aubrey that he was so viewed by the fairer gender. And now, with the added attraction of an earldom to call upon . . . why, his opportunities should be limitless. And, um, it wasn't as if a declaration existed between himself and Grace Woolrich. That which does not exist cannot be shattered, mm? J. Aubrey Whitford cleared his throat. Aubrey, Earl of Whitford, smiled politely as he waited for the introduction that was soon to come.

"Alexandra," Buford Wiscowicz joyously exclaimed.

"Alexandra," Edna Mae Wiscowicz growled.

"Alexandra," Sue Dockery said happily.

"M'lady," Aubrey, Earl of Whitford, intoned a moment before he clicked his heels sharply and then bowed low in greeting.

The young woman came toward the head of the table where Aubrey, Earl of Whitford, had been seated. Her expression was carefully neutral, but her beauty was such that even that was a privilege to gaze upon. A smile from her might have been so overwhelming as to be disruptive of an onlooker's liver functions.

"Your Excellency, allow me to present Miss Alexandra Cowpen," Wiscowicz was saying. J. Aubrey heard the words faintly, as if from a distance. "Alexandra, this noble gentleman is the Earl of Whitford, my dear. From, uh, dear England. You, uh, know?" Buford sounded nonplussed.

The beauteous Alexandra ignored her host's inanity, came forward to stop a few paces before the visiting earl and dropped into a most coyly executed curtsy.

When she lowered her eyes and bowed her head like that J. Aubrey found himself scarcely able to breathe. The sight of her lashes seen long and curling against the pale perfection of her rounded, dimpled, unblemished cheek . . . it was quite enough to take a man's breath away.

She dropped into her curtsy and remained there, giving J. Aubrey the pleasure of a moment in which to observe her without having to rudely stare.

Alexandra Cowpen—how lyrically attractive the name of this rustic burg now seemed—was dark of hair and dark of eye but softly, gently light of form and texture. Her flesh was so pale, in fact, that she seemed ghostly and wraith-like of appearance, an impression that was heightened by the loose, flowing white gown that could have served as a shroud or as a Grecian maiden's dancing costume, as in a May Day celebration, say. J. Aubrey felt his cheeks grow warm and his heartbeat quicken.

Alexandra's cheeks were delicately sunken and her fever-bright eyes set wide and deep. There were hollows at her throat and clavicles, and her figure was lean to the point of being boyish. A man of only ordinary strength might be able to take her up in one hand without need to strain. Yet withal that she was an improbable model for feminine perfection, J. Aubrey discovered that she was indeed that and nothing less. He found himself wanting to take her up in one hand. And into both arms. He found himself wanting to comfort and protect and cherish this exquisitely elfin being who floated where other women walked.

J. Aubrey Whitford was quite smitten.

Aubrey, Earl of Whitford, stared only for the briefest of moments. Then he stepped forward with regal bearing and gentle countenance to place his fingertips to the child-woman's chin and elevate her once more from the deep curtsy to an upright posture. "Charmed," he said softly.

"My apologies for being late, Your Excellency."

"No apology is necessary," he assured her. For that matter, as closely as he could tell, he was for once telling the literal truth. No apology surely could be necessary for the late arrival of one who had been unexpected in the first place. And he could not help but note that no place had been laid at the table to accommodate the presence of Alexandra Cowpen.

Aubrey, Earl of Whitford, reluctantly returned to his own place at the table. He discovered an ally then, and a most surprising one, for it was Edna Mae Wiscowicz who now hurriedly gave up her own position to the distinguished earl's right, gave it up swiftly and without demur. Moments before J. Aubrey would have sworn from her greeting that Edna Mae loathed Alexandra. There were undercurrents flowing here that J. Aubrey failed to comprehend. But to which he found no objection. Not so long as they assured him the close company of this delightful young woman as his dining companion, she who was seated now between himself and Mr. Dockery.

Had he thought before that Edna Mae would not be so boorish as to suggest a companion for the earl? Ha. Bless Edna Mae for proving him a liar in that regard. Bless her twice over for abandoning her seat in favor of Alexandra

Cowpen. Bless one and all for salvaging disaster in the wilderness and bringing him instead to this delectable setting upon the face of the Great American Desert.

Aubrey, Earl of Whitford, could have asked no better than this.

THIRTY-ONE

INATTENTION was not an error a gamesman can ever afford to make. Yet how can one possibly pay heed to the mundane and the ordinary when the luminous and the extraordinary are seated so close by at one's own right hand? How could J. Aubrey possibly monitor his conversations with Wiscowicz and the other gentlemen of Cowpen's Lick when Miss Alexandra Cowpen sat so near that he might have reached out and touched her hand . . . ah, how very much he yearned to touch her hand, and, um, whatever else might prove attainable . . . and yet. . . .

He solved his dilemma by speaking *to* Buford and the other gentlemen but speaking *for* the ears and the enlightenment of Miss Alexandra.

Yes, his captivity among the savages had been emotionally devastating but when seen from this safe and secure perspective could be deemed illuminating as well. Or so he told his eagerly receptive audience.

Yes, he was deeply concerned about the fate of his retainers. They had been, or so the conversation went, separated from him—that is to say, separated from their noble master—at the time of his unfortunate incarceration by the aboriginal natives.

No, he sadly claimed, he as yet had no word of his people's fate. He remained apprehensive.

Yes, he had requested that the military search for them. His hope was that the rescue of his retinue would prove as satisfactory as was the case in his own deliverance from the brink.

No, he was not unduly worried about the personal fortune that was lost along with his retainers. That, after all, was mere gold. The lives of his servants, some of whom had been devoted to him virtually since birth, were far more precious than jeweled trinkets or so easily replaceable specie. Why, after all, gentlemen, a simple message home, sent by fast packet, would alleviate the temporary discommodity caused by one's being among strangers without funds. Or did the gentlemen mean to suggest, ha ha, that he pay in advance for his meals and lodging whilst in residence at Cowpen's Lick, ha ha?

Oh, it was grand—if entirely expected—how these rustics' eyes glistened at the thought of the riches represented by this Earl of Whitford.

J. Aubrey could not help wondering how far he might be able to push this bit of good fortune. A cash advance for the purposes of travel? Crude. Crass. But likely effective. Yet frankly apt to be small potatoes. It was a question to be pondered before any decision need be reached.

And, ahem, a glance now and then to his right, in the direction of Miss Alexandra, proved that haste was not to be desired here in any event.

J. Aubrey smiled with benign good will.

And scattered his spoken seeds upon the soil of these eager listeners' minds. Seed calculated to sprout and to grow. And to be harvested at his leisure when the appropriate methods were decided upon.

In the meanwhile, of course. . . .

He leaned closer to Buford Wiscowicz and confided a tidbit of gossip about Her Majesty, the Queen. Or Great-Aunt Victoria, as Aubrey, Earl of Whitford, knew her.

Wiscowicz listened in wide-eyed wonder. And of course memorized every nuance of word and whisper so as to repeat it afterward. And while he did that Aubrey, Earl of Whitford, sent another speculative sideways glance in the direction of the delectable wraith Miss Alexandra.

This, he thought happily, was everything a dinner party should be.

THIRTY-TWO

J. AUBREY YAWNED into his kerchief, the rudeness of it entirely deliberate. After all, his belly was full and Miss Alexandra Cowpen was already departed. It was time the remainder of the guests received the hint and retired.

Edna Mae Wiscowicz, bless her heart, saw, interpreted, acted. Immediately she began moving through the room, smiling and speaking and ushering people in the direction of the door, all the while thanking them for having come and expressing her great sorrow that the evening could not be prolonged. What the woman lacked in tact she made up in efficiency, J. Aubrey noted with pleasure. Within thirty minutes of Miss Cowpen taking her leave the dining hall was empty save for the Wiscowiczes and their guest of honor.

"Most pleasant," J. Aubrey said languidly.

"Our pleasure," Buford Wiscowicz assured him, although in a tone of voice that lent doubt to the sincerity of the comment. The man had been increasingly withdrawn as the party wore onward. And conversely, J. Aubrey had noted earlier, his sister Edna Mae had been more and more animated and joyous. The seesaw balance between them seemed mildly odd. "Would you excuse me, Your Excellency? I have some things to see to before I retire."

"Mmm, yes. Quite all right, really." J. Aubrey dismissed his host with a limp wave and declined to rise as Wiscowicz bowed out of His Excellency's presence. "Is he all right?" J. Aubrey asked once Buford was out of hearing. "Seems quiet, hmm?"

Edna Mae beamed. "How nice o' you to've noticed, Your Excellency."

"Thank you. But you didn't answer my question, what?"

The lady of the manor—such as it was, which was much for this unspeakably distant place but crudely inelegant by more civilized standards—smiled and leaned forward as if in deep confidentiality. "Could we kinda keep this 'tween the two o' us, Your Excellency?"

"As you wish, madame."

"My brother had him some high hopes that was dashed this evening, Your Excellency. Dashed down an' stomped on."

J. Aubrey lifted an eyebrow but remained silent.

"You seen it for yourself, Your Excellency. That Alexandra was eyein' you, Your Excellency. Has a real case for you, I'd say. And ol' Bufe, that dummy, he'd been wantin' that little filly for himself. Not that I c'n understand it, though I s'pose she's pretty enough in a pasty, washed-out kinda way. Still an' all, Bufe could do better than that. . . . I mean . . . oh, dear. . . ." Her wattled cheeks darkened with a flush of sudden apprehension.

J. Aubrey appreciated the web into which Edna Mae had just entangled herself. After all, she herself had promoted the idea of an interest developing between Miss Cowpen and the Earl of Whitford. An interest which, for the record, J. Aubrey deemed much less obvious than Edna Mae now claimed. Nevertheless, Edna Mae Wiscowicz quite obviously favored the development of an attraction between Alexandra and the Earl of Whitford. Now it appeared that her reason had nothing to do with unsolicited generosity on behalf of a stranger—in which J. Aubrey placed no credence anyway—and much to do with self-interest—which he found to be a most reliable motivating force. For some reason, Edna Mae did not want her brother's infatuation with the young beauty to be reciprocated. Jealousy of her own position? Possible, of course. So why did J. Aubrey not think so? Undeniably he had the feeling there was more to it than that. His point being, in any event, that now Edna Mae had talked herself into a position in which she did not want to say anything disparaging about Alexandra lest the earl be dissuaded from interest. Yet she felt obligated to justify her opposition to Buford's interest. For a moment there, until she caught herself, she'd been on the verge of cattiness and gossip. Too bad she hadn't said the rest of it. Gossip may sometimes carry the most intriguing bits of leverage. . . .

He smiled. Leaned even nearer to his hostess. "This is only between us, remember. You can tell me."

"Oh, there ain't anything more t' tell, Your Excellency. I was just prattlin' on. Bufe tells me I do that too much. I reckon he's right 'bout that."

J. Aubrey shrugged. Straightened. "Correct me if I am mistaken, madame, but when the young lady in question first put in an appearance, I had the distinct impression that you were not pleased."

"Well I wasn't, o' course. But that was 'cause of Bufe. Then I seen that you was interested. And seen what a fine an' handsome pair you an' Alexandra make. An', well, there you have it." She stopped and gave J. Aubrey a speculative look. Whatever she was thinking—the possibilities were limitless—J. Aubrey suspected it was something that would have to do with encouraging the distinguished earl and the local beauty, thus removing opportunity if not temptation from Buford. And that being the case, whatever it was it would be something of which J. Aubrey, the man if not the earl, would thoroughly approve.

J. Aubrey, every inch the earl, coughed delicately into his sleeve and lightly sniffed. "I should like to be shown to my rooms now, if you please." Then he winked at Edna Mae.

The homely woman guffawed. "By damn, Your Excellency, you're all right. C'mon now an' I'll show you t' your digs."

THIRTY-THREE

AUBREY, EARL OF WHITFORD, luxuriated in the bath that had been carried into his room and filled with steaming hot water. It seemed a perfectly idyllic way in which to begin this new day. He slid lower into the sudsy water until he was neck deep, only his leonine head and his somewhat knobby knees protruding above the surface. The heat soaked through flesh and muscle to soothe joint and tendon equally. The sensation was marvelous, particularly so after the filth he'd been required to endure as a captive of those horrendous savages. Why, simply thinking back upon them again was enough to make a gentleman shudder.

He did shudder. Metaphorically if not in actual fact. For a moment, remembering, he felt chilled. He lifted a finger, eyes still closed, and pointed to the surface of the bathwater. A mere moment later he was rewarded with a sound of gentle splashing and a fresh infusion of hot water into the tub. J. Aubrey—that is to say, the Earl of Whitford—permitted himself a tiny smile. And a sigh.

There was, after all, much to be said for the attendance upon one by a well-schooled staff of servants. Of which the Wiscowicz household was generously supplied. And to which a genuine earl of the realm would be quite naturally accustomed. J. Aubrey could do no less than to accept as his due all the attention and assistance implied.

Why, in fact, had he not had the foresight to be born into a situation such as this one? If only he'd thought of it soon enough.

It was, he guessed, close to noon now. But no one in the

household had had the temerity to rouse the earl from his slumbers before he chose to rise.

J. Aubrey had wakened fairly late—not this late of course —and enjoyed the sensations of lying slugabed in broad daylight while downstairs he heard the stirrings of the servants and the louder voices and movements of the family. Buford and Edna Mae had long been about their day's affairs.

At one point J. Aubrey had been tempted to rise and join them. That was when the tantalizing scents of frying bacon reached him. But then, he realized, there truly was no need for the Earl of Whitford to hurry himself in time to make the breakfast table. The Earl of Whitford could choose to have breakfast wait upon his appearance. And so J. Aubrey had turned over, nuzzled deeper into the down-filled pillow upon which his cheek lay and went blissfully back to sleep.

That had been some hours earlier. Now he felt well and truly refreshed, ready first for his bath and then for his breakfast. One of the servants had already departed with the distinguished earl's requirements as to the proper preparation of an egg. Everything would be in readiness when he went downstairs. Whenever he chose for that to be.

Ah, service. Such a grand notion. He really should have thought of this scheme before now.

He waggled his finger again and was rewarded as before with the splash of near-boiling water from kettle to tub.

This afternoon, he decided, he would prevail upon the more than willing Edna Mae to place him in close proximity to Alexandra.

A swift survey of his own emotions and intentions reassured J. Aubrey that his devotion to Miss Grace Woolrich remained undiminished.

But then . . . Miss Grace was not here. Alexandra was.

And there was no understanding between himself and Miss Grace.

Unfortunately.

Why, it would be fortunate indeed if he ever again was able to find her.

At this point, so many days behind, so badly detoured through no fault of his own, there was no way to determine where Miss Grace might now be. Or even which of the many routes away from Texas she may have taken.

His best chance to find her, he now conceded, would be to abandon the hope of direct pursuit and hurry on to San Francisco, where she was almost surely bound.

Hurry, that is, in a manner of speaking.

First there must be a replenishment of his fortunes.

And if this proved to somehow involve Alexandra—J. Aubrey as yet had no inkling what his steps here should entail —well, there would be no harm done.

At this point, however, the only thing he was sure of was that he had, here in Cowpen's Lick, in the unassigned territory that was commonly called Kansas, a most perfect opportunity for profit. Here he had an entire community who believed with all their hearts that their distinguished visitor was none other than a wealthy, titled, line-of-succession nobleman.

No gamesman since the commencement of time had ever had better opportunity to accept fleece from willing sheep.

J. Aubrey grunted softly with true contentment and let himself slide fractionally lower into the copper tub so that even his chin lay submerged in the soothing, rose-scented bathwater.

THIRTY-FOUR

FUNNY, J. Aubrey thought as a pair of servants toweled him dry and a third folded him carefully into the voluminous depths of a robe that would have been large enough to swaddle an ox, funny how ever since his escape from the savages he'd been so intent upon bathing. Immediately at the army post and still here in Cowpen's Lick he was positively anxious to bathe and bathe again. As if there were some taint clinging to him that must be washed away. Yet that was perfectly silly.

"Would there be anything else, suh?"

"Mm, yes. A shave, I should think. If there is anyone in the house with the proper hand for it." After all, with any degree of luck—whether found or fabricated, it mattered little—he would this afternoon convince his new ally Edna Mae to establish renewed contact between himself and Alexandra. A shave certainly seemed in order.

"Yes, suh, as you wish, suh." The servant handling the bathrobe bowed and one of the ones who had been doing the toweling slipped silently away. This was all quite comfortable, J. Aubrey was discovering.

Even so he continued to feel inexplicably . . . soiled. That was the term for it, he concluded. Soiled. After those Indians. . . . He shuddered.

Of course they'd come so near to murdering him. A man never wishes to be that close to his own demise. And yet. . . .

Living in those rude tents under threat of death was hardly J. Aubrey Whitford's first brush with the grim reaper. There had been . . . suffice it to say there had been more

than one disgruntled mark who managed a premature discovery of his own fleecing and more than one husband who
prematurely learned he was wearing the cuckold's horns.
No, this latest was hardly J. Aubrey's first meeting with
death.

But there was something about this experience that was
different from all of those.

It took him a moment to recognize it.

This threat, he realized upon reflection, was so . . .
casual. Dispassionate.

Perhaps that was why it seemed so lastingly frightening.

There had been no heat, no anger present in those Indians when they yawningly considered his murder. No more
so than, indeed no different from, a housewife's consideration of should she wring the red cockerel's neck for dinner
or slice a ham instead. There was no reason why she
shouldn't stew a chicken for dinner. Unless the red cockerel
could be saved for better advantage another time.

That, J. Aubrey realized, was alarmingly like the detached
savagery he'd encountered within those leather lodges.

The Indians had not hated J. Aubrey Whitford. Not in the
slightest. They proposed his murder solely on the grounds
that his flesh was pale where theirs was copper and therefore he was fair game for disposal by whatever method
proved convenient: barter, slaughter, one would serve as
well as the other.

J. Aubrey could not help but shudder as one of Buford
Wiscowicz's servants guided him gently into an upholstered
chair and seated him in readiness for the resident barber.

THIRTY-FIVE

THE RESIDENT BARBER, he was disconcerted to discover, was a young and not unattractive woman, her dusky skin color only a few shades darker than J. Aubrey's own. Enough darker, however, to maintain her in bondage. His discomfort stemmed from the fact that the girl would be working in necessarily intimate proximity to his person while he, fresh from the bath, wore only the loosely draped robe that had been wrapped about him. Worse, she was wearing very little more, her sole—too obviously so—garment being flimsy of construction and haphazardly fitted. While the girl laid out her instruments—set of ivory-handled razors, pair of strops, cakes of scented soap, china mug, astringent toilet waters and so on—J. Aubrey surreptitiously tugged and tucked at the robe in an effort to cover himself as fully as would prove possible.

"Suh?" one of the male servants asked.

"Yes?"

"Does you—I mean, does Yo' Excellency—want me an' Jason to leave so you an' Cleotitia can be alone, suh?"

J. Aubrey blinked. But only until the meaning of the question became clear. "Absolutely not, man. You will stay where you are, please."

"Yes, suh. Whatever you say, suh."

J. Aubrey couldn't be sure. But he thought he could detect a measure of relaxation—relief? most probably—in the set of the girl Cleotitia's shoulders as she poured a tiny measure of water into her mug and began churning the brush about to whip the shaving soap into a froth. He felt no sense of rejection. Nor of disappointment. Her reaction seemed only appropriate. After all, Cleotitia possessed no rights of refusal. Not even about this. It was a situation which J. Aubrey found to be oddly discommoding. After all, even a woman of the night retains the right to refuse the prospective customer's money. Cleotitia hadn't even that modicum of control. The situation, one he had never personally experienced in the past, was definitely off-putting, J. Aubrey found, despite any suppositions of fantasy. He cleared his throat and concentrated his thoughts on more pleasant matters.

Cleotitia, in the meanwhile, proved herself to be shy and quiet but entirely adept as a barber.

The towel she used to soften his stubble was only pleasantly warm, not at all hot enough to make one wince as was the practice with so many professional barbers. And later her touch with the razor was gentle and as delicate as a moth's fluttering wing, yet when he felt of his face it was as smooth as when he'd been a boy, or nearly so.

"You're very good," he idly mentioned as she was cleaning her razors and replacing them into protective cases.

"Thank you, masta." Her voice was as soft as her touch had been.

Masta. Master. Good Lord! No one had ever called him that before.

He found that he didn't like it.

Your Excellency, Your Royal Highness, Sir, Sire . . . all those titles he not only accepted, he reveled in them. Those were part and parcel of the game, proof of his mastery over some unsuspecting mark. Those were, frankly, very good fun.

But . . . master? Spoken in all seriousness? In all *involuntary* seriousness?

The idea of it left something of a bad taste in his mouth.

He had no idea what Aubrey, Earl of Whitford, should think or feel as concerned this subject. But J. Aubrey Whitford found the whole thing to be entirely discomfiting. And therefore best put out of mind.

He scowled and cleared his throat and ordered all the servants, female and male alike, away from him, choosing to dress himself now even though half an hour earlier he had been quite looking forward to the silly, snobbish, foppish luxury of having a body servant to pull his stockings on for him.

"Tell the cook I shall expect my breakfast in twenty minutes," he instructed, almost having to force himself to resume his role as earl and potential heir.

"Yes, suh, whatever you say, suh," and the servants all bowed their way out of the great man's presence.

THIRTY-SIX

THE RESIDENTS of this ignorant backwater for miles and miles around seemed intent upon turning the entire countryside inside out in honor of the most distinguished personage any single one of them was apt to meet in his or her lifetime. While Aubrey, Earl of Whitford, lay in slumber the folk had buzzed and scurried like so many ants, preparing an impromptu gala in his honor. After all, J. Aubrey realized, none of them knew when the noble visitor might choose to take his leave from Cowpen's Lick and its environs. They had to act quickly while they still had the chance to do so.

None of them, of course, was aware that the visitor himself would have been incapable of granting them information about his plans, about how long he would remain among them. As quickly as leave-taking was to his advantage, he would go. As quickly as he'd devised a score and milked this opportunity to whatever extent proved possible. Hopefully no sooner. After all, one's acceptance as a legitimate earl of the British realm was hardly an everyday occurrence; it was due a certain measure of respect and appreciation from the gamesman as well as from his marks.

J. Aubrey felt the weight of that responsibility as following breakfast he joined Buford Wiscowicz in the library—he had no idea what it might be that Buford did for a living, but whatever it was seemed to involve no labor and little need for absence from the house—and accepted a mellow brandy from his host. There was no sign now of Edna Mae although she had sat with him through breakfast and informed him about the plans for the evening gala.

"Anything you need, Your Excellency? Anything at all?"

"Nothing at the moment, Mr. Wiscowicz, thank you."

"You think of anything, Your Excellency, you open right up an' tell me. An' I mean that. Anything."

"Nothing, thanks," J. Aubrey repeated.

"Anything," Buford muttered. J. Aubrey wondered how heavily the man had been into the brandy thus far. Of course the hour had advanced well into the post-noon by this time. There was no reason why a gentleman of leisure shouldn't allow himself a tipple or two now. "Any ol' thing, eh?"

J. Aubrey, or rather the earl, ventured a few remarks about literature, a few more about art, architecture, sculpture, dance. Not that he was versed on any of these but they seemed interests that would be appropriate to an earl, and they were the sort of thing that one hears at least a bit about when living in a city. He was able to discuss them.

Buford Wiscowicz, it proved, was not able to do so. The man was unquestionably wealthy. He owned land and slaves. He was a man of leisure. He was not, J. Aubrey concluded, a gentleman. And although surely there must somewhere be a subject or subjects that Buford would have been able to intelligently discuss, Aubrey, Earl of Whitford, failed to touch upon it or them during that largely one-sided conversation in the Wiscowicz library.

After a bit J. Aubrey gave up on his attempts at conversation. He settled for wandering over to a window and peering out in solitude and silence.

The scene before him was without particular interest. Slaves and white laborers alike were engaged in erecting trestle tables and a brush arbor in preparation for the evening's gala. Beyond the al fresco dining grounds he could see smoke rising into the air from a pit where quantities of timber were being reduced to bright-hot coals and, close by, smoke from other cooking pits where the coals thus formed were being put to use. At those pits there were white-clad, sweat-sheened Negroes turning massive spits to roast a beef here, a pair of hogs there, what appeared to be a sheep on yet another spit. With all of that food in preparation, surely the United States Army had been invited to attend this evening. Or such of its members as happened at the moment to be between Missouri and Santa Fe. Surely otherwise there could not be enough civilized population found throughout all the Great American Desert to consume all of this.

Not that J. Aubrey objected. If it proved true that every white person in the area were drawn to the Wiscowicz manor tonight then it must necessarily follow that Alexandra Cowpen would be among the guests. He found himself hoping that this would be the case.

And in the meanwhile . . . he sighed. In the meanwhile he truly needed to give serious thought to his own immediate prospects. Serious thought and serious planning as well.

It is a singular thing to find oneself in a situation virtually without limits. He was widely known and thoroughly accepted as the Earl of Whitford. This was, he conceded, a gamesman's dream come true.

It was like a small and grubby-faced boy being left alone overnight in a confectioner's shop. It was a safe-breaker being given a passkey capable of opening any box ever made. It was a riverboat gambler being gifted with second sight. It was all those things and more.

But . . . he didn't know what he wanted to *do* with his earldom now that he had it.

How best to capitalize? How best to milk these people? Should he try to spread the opportunity far and wide? Or concentrate simply on Buford instead? For that matter, what need for great and gaudy sums could an earl have? And how might he convince someone here—Buford, whomever— that they should force him to accept such munificent sums from them?

The truth, he was beginning to recognize, was that his opportunity here was so grandiose, so without limitation, that it fair frightened him with the sheer enormity of it. This was his chance to make history. A whispered sort of history, true. The sort that would be appreciated by only a select few practitioners of the gamesman's art. But history nonetheless.

J. Aubrey found his heart beating at a mad rate as the combination of worry and exhilaration warred within his breast. Worry that he might fail to make the most of this rare stroke of monumental fortune. Exhilaration too, though, in his appreciation of it.

One thing was definite, however. He would not, absolutely would not consider, leaving Cowpen's Lick without burdening himself quite heavily with gold. Or with some suitable equivalent.

If he didn't run *some* scam on these people he would never be able to forgive himself.

THIRTY-SEVEN

COUNTRY FOLK are easily amused. Or so J. Aubrey concluded during the course of the gala that was staged in his honor.

Unlike the previous evening's dinner which had welcomed only a select few of the area's civic and/or fiscal leaders and more in line with the Y'all Come spirit of the initial welcoming celebration, this evening's party was a Come One Come All affair that was not limited to the upper crust but extended to the plebeian crumbs as well. Or thus, um, so to speak, J. Aubrey wryly determined.

In any event, the affair was attended by every bit as many as had shown up for the speech-making upon the grand earl's arrival.

Once again the grounds were festooned with red and white and blue bunting, streamers and cockades. Vast quantities of foods were distributed by Negro servants. Kegs of beer were breached and more piled ready for service when those ran dry. Smaller casks of bitingly hard cider were on hand as were quantities of root beer and sarsaparilla for the timid. In addition to the selection of meats there were tubs of kraut, bushels of corn dodgers, loaves of crusty bread by the dozens, kegs of pickles and crocks of preserves. For a hungry man the Wiscowicz yard would have seemed a godsend.

In addition to the patriotic decorations—which J. Aubrey still failed to comprehend, considering that the earl was of supposed British origin—the trees and nearby structures and indeed a good many additional poles emplaced for the specific purpose were hung with paper lanterns that spread a soft yellow glow upon the scene, each of the lanterns illumined not with cheap, guttering candles but by scores and scores of small lamps burning the best quality whale oil.

During the afternoon a dance ground had been laboriously cleared, swept, watered and tamped so that by night the dried, crusted surface was smooth and hard and nearly free of dust.

An orchestra—of sorts—played close by to the dance ground. The concatenation of instruments available in this isolated backwater, and the alleged musicians to man them, provided what might best be described as a nontraditional melding of orchestral tones, leaning heavily toward wind and percussion rather than string. Assuming, that is, that one would choose to place the concertina in the category of wind instruments. Or might those be regarded as reeds? J. Aubrey was undecided on that point. Regardless, the assemblage included three concertinas, two bugles, one cornet, one French horn, one bassoon, four harmonicas, two drums, one cymbal, one piccolo, two fiddles and several gourd rattles. Also one upended steel tub which, incredibly, was a string instrument—J. Aubrey would not have believed this had he not personally observed it at close and critical length. Possessing a limber upright member and a single stout cord, the washtub gave off a one-note thrumming noise that was in truth not unlike the sound of a note from a stringed bass instrument. The orchestra thus formed played with much more gusto than skill, but they did produce sounds that had a recognizably repeatable pattern or rhythm and thus served adequately for those who chose to dance to this music. Dancers who, J. Aubrey noted, were no more gifted in that art than were the musicians in theirs. In fact, dancers and music seemed to be well and comfortably suited to one another and thus probably should be considered an unqualified success.

What with liquor, food and dancing a good time was being had by most if not quite by all. Certainly the guests appeared to be enjoying themselves with raucous abandon. The only party present who was not was the Earl of Whitford. Or so J. Aubrey glumly believed.

This distress he attributed to the absence from the party of Alexandra Cowpen, who had made no appearance throughout the late afternoon, early evening or now into the night. The Earl of Whitford sat in the throne-like chair that had been placed on a slightly raised platform adjacent to the dance area and nursed a noggin of tangy cider.

"Would you care to dance, Your Excellency?"

He blinked, startled out of his reverie. Sue Dockery had swirled to a panting halt before him, her eyes bright and sparkling with the unpent joys of the night—or perhaps from the ingestion of a quantity of spirits—her cheeks aglow with the rosy coloration imparted by healthy exertion.

The lady's gown was cut quite low. And she was, as stated, gasping for breath, her chest thus heaving and her pulse racing. The combination proved of irresistible interest. J. Aubrey's eyes were drawn inevitably to the display that was being presented to him.

His thoughts were drawn quite as inevitably to a recognition of what else was being presented.

Mrs. Dockery was, after all, fully aware of her own appearance. J. Aubrey had known countless women who professed innocence in such matters. He had never known one who was, however, so innocent. In particular not any woman already familiar with the marital couch.

No, Mrs. Dockery intended to make an offer that included more than a dance.

And yesterday J. Aubrey, that is to say the Earl of Whitford, undoubtedly would have accepted her offer without qualm.

But now. . . . Now, he realized with no small degree of surprise, now he had no inclination to tiptoe out into the shadows with Dockery's young and pretty wife.

It wasn't that he was so enamored of Alexandra Cowpen

that he would accept no substitute. Hardly that. Nor that he was as yet so committed to Grace Woolrich that he felt obligated to preserve himself for her alone. Certainly not that either since it was undetermined whether he would ever again find his dear and beloved Grace. And, admittedly, he would be quite willing to dally with Alexandra in Grace's absence.

So why this uncharacteristic reluctance to engage in a little touch-and-tickle with Mrs. Dockery?

He grunted unhappily and squirmed upon his chair as if a host of ants had just that moment infested it. "I, uh," he cleared his throat, "not now, mm? Later, per'aps."

The lady seemed surprised. But no more so than he, although he could not tell her that. "As you wish, Your Excellency."

"Yes, well, mm, thank you."

She curtsied, waved gaily across the dance space toward her husband and scampered off to meet him, her skirts flying and her step light and cheerful.

Behind her J. Aubrey felt considerably less cheer than the gay young wife exhibited.

Whatever was it, he wondered, that was distressing him so? Whatever it was he wished it would go away.

He might have pondered the question further had not Alexandra chosen that moment to make, as before, a belated appearance at the earl's party.

And as before, her arrival brightened the assemblage as if the number of lamps were suddenly doubled.

Aubrey, Earl of Whitford, rose to greet her, and his spirits rose as well.

Whatever it was that had been nagging him could well be put in abeyance for the time being.

"Miss Cowpen." He bowed. "May I have the honor of this dance?"

She blushed and placed her hand trustingly into his. Ah,

he thought, foolish girl to be so trusting. How foolish. How convenient.

He smiled and accepted her fingertips onto the back of his hand and imperiously called to the orchestra for a waltz.

This, he determined, was more like it. This diversion was precisely what he required to heal his troubled emotions. And smiling he led the beauteous lass in a whirl.

THIRTY-EIGHT

APART FROM THE FACT that the orchestra was only marginally familiar with the requirements of a waltz, and apart from the fact that Alexandra seemed wholly unfamiliar with the movements of one, the dance in J. Aubrey's judgment was going quite well indeed.

At least the musicians banged and wheezed and clattered in mostly the right manner, and Alexandra swayed and swirled along with him, bumping against him every now and then. But that he felt to be no drawback whatsoever.

Predictably, the dance floor cleared immediately when the Earl of Whitford assumed his place upon it for the first time that evening, and J. Aubrey and Alexandra were ringed by admiring onlookers who were enjoying the sight of a titled nobleman dancing with one of their own.

Unpredictably, the pleasure of the dance lasted for only a few minutes.

It wasn't that the orchestra was unwilling to play on nor that J. Aubrey or Alexandra either one chose to stop.

Rather, a third party intruded upon the occasion.

Rudely.

One moment J. Aubrey was holding Alexandra as close to him as was seemly—and indeed a trifle closer, his reasoning being that no one in Cowpen's Lick would know the current trends and fashions of Europe, not any more than J. Aubrey would himself, but there was no reason why he shouldn't invent a new mode of dance that would place the lovely girl tight against him on frequent occasion—the next he was engaged in a turn that included no partner. Alexandra had quite disappeared from within his arms. And abruptly at that.

"Here now," he protested, turning to see a tall, gray-haired gentleman of middle years and distinguished bearing who had J. Aubrey's recent dance partner firmly gripped at the upper arm. The man seemed intent upon dragging the girl away.

"Daddy!" Alexandra yelped.

"Don't defy me, girl. You knew not to come here. You did it anyway. Now suffer the consequences. Go home, child. This instant, go home." He raised an open hand as if to slap her, and Alexandra trembled, bursting into tears.

"What do you think you're doing, man?" J. Aubrey loudly growled. "Do you have any idea who you've accosted here?"

"Damn right I do," the gentleman said, looking at the Earl of Whitford for the first time. "I'm collecting my own daughter and sending her back to her room, sir. Where she was supposed to be ever since dinner this evening at my specific instruction. No offense to you, mister. Or earl. Whatever the hell you're supposed to be called. No offense to you. But I'll not have any daughter of mine seen at an affair put on by those . . . those . . . *creatures* over there." He pointed an accusing—although accusing of what J. Aubrey was uncertain—finger in the direction of Buford and Edna Mae Wiscowicz. Until now they had been basking in the admiration of their neighbors as host and hostess to the distinguished personage, as well as providers of this feast and festivity.

Cowpen turned back to his daughter. "You heard me, young lady. Home. This instant."

"But Daddy," she wailed.

"Now!"

Alexandra gave J. Aubrey, that is the Earl of Whitford, a look of utter mortification, gathered her skirts into both hands and went running off the dance floor and into the night, quickly disappearing beyond the line of paper lanterns and away out of sight.

Cowpen, his expression determined but no longer hostile, turned to J. Aubrey and bowed. "My apologies, sir. Good night." And without another word he too took his departure, albeit at a more dignified pace than Alexandra had adopted.

"Hummph!" J. Aubrey snorted.

All around the party-goers were staring at their shoes, into the sky, at each other's backsides, anywhere but into the center of the dance floor where their entire community had just been embarrassed.

All of them save Buford and Edna Mae who, equally as horrified as Alexandra had been, now were rushing with squeals of loud apology and widespread hands to their most distinguished guest of honor.

Damned odd this entire, sordid thing, J. Aubrey thought glumly.

He allowed the Wiscowiczes to yammer out all the obligatory and essentially meaningless apologies, but he paid scant attention to anything either of them was saying.

The point was that he'd been miserable earlier. Then so briefly pleased. And now he was most thoroughly miserable once again.

The major difference between the way he'd felt earlier and the way he felt now, he decided, was that before he hadn't known why he felt so damn-all down. At least now he could attach a reason to the mood. Small comfort that.

With a resigned sigh he waved the Wiscowiczes into silence and plodded back to his dais and throne. Or, um, platform and chair. At the moment, though, even that conceit was able to give him no pleasure.

And he *still* didn't know how best he should fill his pockets before he made his departure from Cowpen's Lick, an occasion he was beginning to think could come none too soon to suit him.

THIRTY-NINE

J. AUBREY wasn't sure how long these affairs were supposed to last—a reasonably similar event he'd observed while in Texas recently had gone on until there were no participants remaining upright to carry on—but this particular one petered out and died before midnight, probably as a result of the general humiliation that had been imposed upon the populace by Alexander Cowpen. No one save the Wiscowiczes had seemed all that interested in maintaining a facade of gaiety. Certainly the Earl of Whitford was not.

So now J. Aubrey sat morose and restless in a borrowed dressing gown. From the upper-floor window of his borrowed suite of rooms he could look down upon the remnants of the prematurely defunct party. There were very nearly as many people down there now, he saw, as there had been during the gala, the difference between them being hue more than head count. The Wiscowicz servants had been summoned out to clean up after their betters and now were laboring with commendable enthusiasm toward that end, their zeal at the moment being concentrated on cleaning up any and everything that remained on each of the roasting spits, on every platter, from each food tub and out of all the kegs and casks and hogsheads. Enthusiastic? Ravenous would seem more in order if judged from appearances alone. Although of course that could not be so. The Wiscowiczes were wealthy and more than capable of feeding their many servants.

Still and all there was no denying the near frantic intensity with which the foods and beverages disappeared. J. Aubrey frowned as he looked down upon the scene. It was . . . unseemly . . . in so opulent a household.

Not that it was any of his business, though. Nor did he know enough about the subject to form intelligent opinion about it. He himself had nothing to do with the peculiar institution. Never had. In fact, his only real contact with any member of the Negro race had been with the woman Jeptha. And she could hardly be considered a good example inasmuch as she had scarpered off away from her lawful master at the earliest opportunity, abandoning the benefits of civilization in exchange for the savagery of those horrid Indians. So, no, Jeptha could not be considered a source of knowledge about the subject.

The best thing for J. Aubrey to do, he concluded, and for the Earl of Whitford also, was simply to ignore all of that and concentrate instead on that which did concern him: i.e., how best to separate the good folk of Cowpen's Lick from a hefty chunk of their worldly wealth.

He stared out of the bedroom window and tried to think upon that question. He might have been successful too. Except that he kept seeing all those people down there pushing and shoving at one another, grabbing for any shred of meat or globule of fat and stuffing whatever came to hand into their mouths. The sight was depressing enough to make him shudder.

"I believe I would like a brandy now," he said softly.

Immediately there was a muted scuffle of bare feet moving on a hardwood floor and the click of glass upon glass. A small snifter one quarter full with amber liquid was placed into his hand as if by magic. J. Aubrey smelled of the brandy for a moment, then tentatively tasted it. He nodded. "Shouldn't you be down there with everyone else?"

"No, suh. I b'long here t'night, suh."

"As you wish." He had another sip of the brandy. And realized that he'd been wrong. The man was not doing as he wished. Whatever that may or may not have been. Instead

the servant was doing as he must. J. Aubrey raised his eyes
and for the first time looked closely into the blankly unemo-
tional features of the man who at least for tonight was his
own personal body servant. "Are you hungry?"

"No, suh."

"Those people down there look hungry."

The Negro squirmed a little and shook his head.

"Never mind then." J. Aubrey tasted of the brandy again.
"What's your name?"

"Ark, suh. Short for Archimedes."

"Do you know who Archimedes was?"

"No, suh." The man looked distinctly uncomfortable.

J. Aubrey gave up the unwelcomed questioning and con-
templated the inside of the brandy snifter instead. When he
looked up again Ark had silently withdrawn into the shadows. As if in escape? Or as much of one as was permissible?
J. Aubrey suspected so. He drank off the rest of his brandy
and refused another when Ark swiftly but quietly brought
the decanter. "No, thank you."

"Yes, suh."

J. Aubrey sighed. He was tired. But not sleepy. He didn't
really want to go to bed. Didn't want to sit by this damned
window and stare out at a bunch of slaves feeding like animals either. Didn't want to read. Didn't want to dance.
Didn't want to . . .

What he did feel like, he supposed, was another bath. But
that was silly. He'd had a bath just hours ago.

Damn fate anyway. He hadn't wanted to be here to begin
with. Hadn't wanted ever to leave New York and all the tried
and true scams. Hadn't wanted to come to this awful, uncivilized country where none of the rules were as they should
be. Damn it. He—

A tapping at the door jarred him out of his dark thoughts.

J. Aubrey lifted a finger toward the closed door. Ark
bowed once in his direction and went to the door. He
opened it and the pretty barber from earlier slipped inside.

She whispered something to Ark, and the man nodded. He turned to J. Aubrey. "I be going now, suh. Unless you need me?"

"That will be fine, Ark. Thank you."

The man hesitated for so brief a moment that J. Aubrey might have been mistaken about it. Then he bowed low and withdrew, pulling the door closed behind him.

The girl—J. Aubrey tried to recall her name but could not, something odd was all that he could remember it to be—slid the bolt closed behind Ark, leaving only herself within the suite to tend to the grand earl's needs. She seemed frightened, J. Aubrey thought. Frightened and as timid as a doe stepping from the protections of the forest into the dangers of an open, peaceful glade.

"Is something wrong . . . ," now that his tongue was in motion the name came onto it quite on its own, "Cleotitia?"

She shook her head.

"Well then. . . ." He didn't know what else to say. Let his voice die away. He looked out of the window and down. It had been only moments since Ark left, he thought, but there the servant was, outside on the grounds already and breaking into a run to claim his share of whatever might be left on the spits.

J. Aubrey heard a whisper of sound and looked around again.

Cleotitia still stood near the door. But the sound he'd heard was the faint rustle of cloth falling. The girl had dropped her dress from her shoulders and allowed it to slither to the floor. As before, she had been wearing nothing else.

Now she stood in the uncertain, flickering lamplight with her hands shyly clasped and her eyes cast downward, unable to meet the white master's gaze but quite patently instructed to make the visitor thoroughly comfortable in this house. Her complexion, pale in daylight, was in the yellow glow of the short trimmed lamps a bright, burnished copper accented with deep shadows and hard angles. Her frame was light and she was spare of flesh. She was perfectly immobile and—he was loath to admit it but could not do otherwise—exquisitely lovely. She might have been a still-life painting or a statue of a nude—either of those would have allowed for an appreciative appraisal of her beauty without the intrusion of lust—save for the frantically quick flutter of pulse that beat in the hollow of her throat.

She was, J. Aubrey realized, more totally his than any woman ever had been. As completely—and as impersonally—his as a suit of clothing or a drinking vessel. He could do with her, quite literally, anything he wished. *Any*thing.

He cleared his throat and looked quickly away, a flush of heat surging through his neck and into his ears.

"Get dressed, child. Please."

FORTY

THE GIRL was weeping almost hysterically now, sobbing and shuddering and straining to breathe in great gulps of air in between times. J. Aubrey found the brandy decanter and poured a tot of the fiery liquor. He pushed the snifter into Cleotitia's hands and held it to her lips until she consented to drink.

"It's all right, you know. I'm not going to hurt you."

"But I was told . . . I thought . . ."

"Never mind what you thought or what you were told. I'm not going to hurt you."

"My beau . . . he was scared you . . ."

"It's all right. Drink that. It'll calm you down. Then you can go find him, tell him that nothing happened."

"Oh, no, suh, I couldn't do that. I couldn't leave outa here tonight or Masta Buford'd have me whipped."

"Do you mean . . . actually . . . with a *whip?*"

She gave him an odd look. "But of course." The idea seemed quite matter-of-fact to Cleotitia. Quite perfectly appalling to J. Aubrey. He was the one who shuddered at the thought, not she.

"I was told to spend the night, suh. I can't leave till mornin' or I be in big trouble."

"That won't be any problem," he said. And if he had any privately held reservations about that assurance, well, what was a man supposed to do when he was locked up overnight with an attractive girl who could not refuse him? J. Aubrey Whitford had no desire to be known for long-suffering, nor for any other of the so-called sterling qualities. Dammit.

"Thank you, suh."

He grunted.

"I was real sorry your evenin' was mussed up, suh," Cleo-titia said after a bit, as if she were uncomfortable in the intimacy of silence.

"Mm. Saw that, did you?"

"Yes, suh."

"Nobody would tell me why the fellow would do such a thing as that."

"Suh?"

"Cowpen. You know. Alexandra's father. No one would tell me why he should be so exercised. After all, I was only dancing with the girl." And if he'd had other hopes, well, that was neither here nor there at the moment; certainly it had nothing to do with a perfectly innocent waltz conducted in full view of several hundreds of wide-eyed guests.

"You don' know, suh?"

"I believe I said that, didn't I?" he snapped.

Cleotitia jumped as though he'd just struck her. Certainly she acted as if she expected to be struck.

"Sorry," he muttered. "But no, I have no idea why Cowpen would so strongly object to me dancing with his daughter. Like I told you, no one would explain it. They only skirted round the issue whenever I asked."

"All us niggers knows that, suh."

"Oh?"

"Hasn't nothing t' do with you, suh. It's with Masta Buford an' Mistress Edda Mae. Mistuh Cowpen don' want his girl round them."

"Really."

"Yes, suh. Mistuh Cowpen, he a abo . . . abo . . . abo-lition man, suh. One of them as says slaving is wrong, you see."

"An abolitionist."

"Yes, suh. An' Masta Buford an' Mistress Edda Mae, they

come here so's they can get folk here t' be on they side an' all keep slaves like in the south, suh."

"I don't understand," J. Aubrey admitted.

"Can you keep a secret, suh? I mean, I wouldn' say nothing but for you bein' from some other country so you don' got nothing to say 'bout things here. You won' care or nothing. But, I dunno, it kinda explains 'bout Mistuh Cowpen."

"I can keep a secret, Cleotitia."

"Yes, suh. Well the thing is, Mistuh Cowpen an' his kind, they was here first, you see. Not supposed to be no settlement round here, not yet, but they come in an' was here first. Say they wanta make sure when this Kansas is made a . . . what d'you call it? Not a state but somethin' else."

"Territory?"

"That's it, suh. They say when this Kansas gets made a territory it gonna be free ground. Place where even a nigger can't be no slave, suh."

"The place I'm from is free," J. Aubrey mentioned. He was thinking of New York but presumed the same statement would apply to England as well. Or did it? It wasn't a question he'd ever particularly cared about in the past. Now for some reason he did, at least insofar as New York's laws on the subject were concerned. He was finding himself, in fact, rather proud of the dear old place at the moment.

"Masta Buford, he in politics back in 'Bama or some such place, suh."

"That's where you're from, Cleotitia? Alabama?"

"No, suh. I from Miss'sippi. Ark from 'Bama, though. That's my beau, that fine man Ark. We're gonna be married, sometime we find somebody can read for us from the book."

"I don't understand," J. Aubrey said. "If Buford is from Alabama but you aren't, how did you come to be here with him?"

"Oh, Masta Buford, he didn' own but a few folk where he come from. All the rest was given over to him, suh, so that him an' Mistress Edda Mae could come here an' do the poli-tickin' to make this Kansas a slave-holdin' place, suh."

"Really."

"Yes, suh. Bunch o' politician men from all over, suh, they give Masta Buford what he needs t' do that. Niggers, money, whatever."

"Money too?"

"Oh, yes, suh. Ark, he been with Masta Buford right along, not like me. Masta Buford wasn't no rich man back there in 'Bama. My masta had a finer house than him then. More niggers too. My masta give me to Masta Buford be-cause his wife get after him, catch him sneaking me up the back stairs an' get all over him. Next thing I know, I been given over to Masta Buford and told I his from now on. Signed paper on it, they did. Masta Buford showed me."

J. Aubrey frowned. But there wasn't much that could be said about it. However loathsome it might sound to him for one human to hold right and title to another, the entire transaction was legal and aboveboard.

"You say all these people were donated and money too?"

"Oh, yes, suh. Masta Buford and Mistress Edda Mae put on a big show, make everybody round here see how grand it is t' own niggers. That's why they have you in an' show you off, suh."

The girl blushed. He hadn't known—that is of course they would; but he hadn't thought about it; exactly—the truth was that J. Aubrey hadn't known that Negroes could blush. Really he didn't know very much about them at all. Never needed nor particularly desired to. But Cleotitia definitely blushed now, her complexion becoming a trifle darker and being suffused with a dusky rose tint.

"I shouldn' say that 'bout a fine gentleman such as you, suh. I mean, you all noble an' everything. I know they'd o' been proud to have you in an' show you off even if they wasn't wanting to impress all these other white folk an' get them folk to thinking how they do 'stead of how Mistuh Cowpen an' his people do."

"I'll be damned," J. Aubrey whispered. "In the middle of a political scrap, eh?"

"Don' feel bad, suh. I shouldn't o' said nothing."

He smiled. "Cleotitia, I can't begin to tell you how pleased I am that you did tell me. Now I understand a great deal more than I ever could have if we hadn't had this little conversation. You, um, wouldn't happen to know anything about Miss Alexandra Cowpen too, would you?"

"No, suh. If Mistuh Cowpen kept any niggers I'd know anything that happen in that house. But he don't. So I can't tell you nothing 'bout her 'cept what I seen down there t'night." She frowned, paused.

"Yes?" J. Aubrey prompted.

"I heard . . . mind, suh, I don' eavesdrop on nobody . . . but I couldn't help but overhear somethin' one time, suh . . . I think maybe Masta Buford wants Miss Alexandra for a wife. I think he smitten with her, suh. An' I think Mistress Edda Mae don' like her none. She jealous, though, nothin' t' do with Miss Alexandra. Mistress Edda Mae don' want nobody in Masta Buford's bed."

"Not even you, Cleotitia?"

"Oh, not none of us darkies, suh. Masta Buford, he wouldn' even think o' nothing like that. Why, he just as soon take any other farm kind o' animal to bed as a nigger, suh. One be the same as another to him that way. No, suh, he don' bed no niggers. I safe from him. An' now that I'm safe from you too I hope I still be a virgin when me an' Ark find somebody can read the words an' marry us together."

"It's a preacher you need then?"

"Oh, suh, be no preachers for nigger slaves. Just anybody as can read an' would say the words. That's all we need. Ark, he got the book. Just need somebody knows how to read from it."

J. Aubrey chuckled. "Cleotitia, do you think it possible

that Ark might be the, um, person who comes to wait on me in the morning?"

"Likely, suh. Why?"

"If there's some way for you to get word to him, girl, why don't you suggest he bring his book along with him then. I can read rather well, if I do say so myself." He grinned at her.

"Suh? A fine, powerful white man like you do somethin' like that for us?"

"I daresay I shall enjoy it," the Earl of Whitford responded with a twinkle in his eye. "But for right now, dear, I need to sit quietly by myself for a while. I have some ideas I need to ponder." He laughed. "Thanks to you, my dear. Go on now. Try to get some rest. After all, child, tomorrow is to be your wedding day. And if I'm not mistaken, tomorrow shall be my lucky day as well. So off with you now. Go on. Scat."

FORTY-ONE

"WISCOWICZ."

"Yes, Your Excellency?"

"I don't suppose there's been any word yet about my retainers or my luggage, mm?"

"No, Your Excellency. Nothing."

J. Aubrey scowled, went back to the newspaper, a month-old copy of the *New Orleans Intelligencer* that was open in his lap. He, Buford and Edna Mae were having a quiet afternoon in the parlor, the Earl of Whitford reading, Edna Mae tatting a doily and Buford dozing behind the pretext of reading a volume of poetry.

"Is anything wrong, Your Excellency? You look worried."

J. Aubrey hesitated. Just a little, the delay almost—but not quite—imperceptible. "No. Course not."

"All right then," Buford said. He went back to pretending to read his book. But then J. Aubrey always had considered Buford to be a trifle thick in more than body alone.

Edna Mae frowned. "You sure 'bout that, Your Excellency?"

J. Aubrey glowered at her, and she quickly dropped her gaze back in the direction of her tatting. Her fingers flew about the homey task.

Ten or so minutes later J. Aubrey once again broke the silence. "What is the date, pray?"

Buford snorted as his eyes popped open. He looked disoriented and no doubt was. Edna Mae said, "Thursday."

"I meant the calendar date."

"Bufe?"

Buford rubbed his puffy, reddened eyes and tried without

much success to swallow back a yawn. "Mmmph. Sorry."
He shivered and pushed himself upright in the chair. Until
then he'd been gradually slumping deeper and deeper into
the upholstery, his chin sinking to his chest and his breathing becoming stentorian. Now he seemed to be finding it
difficult to reclaim his faculties. "Sorry," he repeated. "What
was that again?"

"His Excellency wants t' know what date it is, Bufe."

"Mmmph, yes, um . . . September, um, twenty-some-
thing? I think so. Long 'bout that, anyway." He lifted a hand
and rubbed his eyes again, scrubbed his lips with the back
of the same hand, turned it over and belched into the palm
of it. Classy fellow, J. Aubrey thought.

"Was there something . . . ?" Edna Mae started, stumbled, stopped.

"No. Not at all." J. Aubrey looked down at the newspaper.
Grunted. Looked up again. "You wouldn't know how long it
takes for mail to travel from here to Washington City, would
you?"

"No. Sorry."

"New York then?"

"Sorry. We've never sent nothing there. Was there something . . . ?"

"No. Never mind." He bent to the newspaper again.
Waited. After a bit when once more he looked up he discovered that Edna Mae continued to watch him closely. "What I
am attempting to discern," the earl said, "is the approximate
amount of time one can reasonably expect for a roundabout
of communication between here and London."

"Oh dear," Edna Mae said.

"Damn long time, that's how long," Buford said with a
snort that had nothing to do with an afternoon's nap.
"Damn long."

J. Aubrey grunted. Re-read a not particularly interesting
article in the newspaper. Turned to the next page and ex-

amined it at length before he looked up again. "Not more than a month, surely," he suggested.

"Lot more'n a month," Buford said.

"Oh, I should think longer," Edna Mae agreed.

The Earl of Whitford grimaced. Went back to his paper.

"Is there something wrong with that, Your Excellency?"

"Course not," he growled and snapped the flimsy newsprint impatiently as if to put an end to such silliness.

"Sorry, Your Excellency."

"Sorry."

He grunted.

Twenty minutes later he spoke again. "Have to punch up the lads in uniform, eh? Shake them around a bit. Get 'em to finding my luggage, what? It's important, don't you see. If it takes all that long . . . never mind. Just see to it that the army recovers my things, that's all. Send someone at once to give that imbecile Dinwittie a reminder, eh? Most important, man. Stress that to him. I must have that luggage back."

"Really?"

"Don't question me, Wiscowicz. Simply do as I ask. Nothing difficult about that, is there? Now send someone."

"Yes, of course, Your Excellency. Right away." Buford heaved himself out of his chair, but Edna Mae was quicker. She was up and away before her brother was well started.

J. Aubrey conspicuously watched Edna Mae out of the room before he added for Buford's ears alone, "By the way, old fellow. Meant to thank you for last night's, um, amusements. Dandy creature that little nigra gal. Wouldn't mind having her every night. In fact, I've been pleased with all the servants you've given me. Good of you is what I say. Have to do something for you sometime, what? ha ha." He winked. And again went back to reading the newspaper.

That, he thought, should launch the ship rather nicely.

FORTY-TWO

"GOOD NIGHT, Wiscowicz, Miss Wiscowicz. Good night to you both."

"G'night, Your Excellency."

"Good night, sire."

Edna Mae with her escort of lamp-bearing servants passed on down the hall to the room she was using. J. Aubrey suspected that the suite given to him was normally Edna Mae's. But he was not in the slightest inclined to suggest she return to it, with or without him remaining in residence. An earl was, after all, entitled to the best these colonial rustics could offer. Particularly so in that their desire was to use his presence to their own ends. Turnabout is always fair play.

The Earl of Whitford, that is to say J. Aubrey, hid a smile in the shadows of the upstairs corridor. There was an old saying to the effect that one cannot con an honest man. J. Aubrey wouldn't know, never having found one to try the theory against. And the Wiscowiczes would not qualify as his first. Imagine: someone wanting to use him to create credence and respectability for themselves. He found the irony of that to be perfectly delicious.

"I say, Wiscowicz."

"Yes, Your Excellency?"

"You haven't forgotten, um . . . ?" He winked and pointed toward the door to his suite.

Buford, earthy fellow that he was, chuckled. "I didn't forget, Your Excellency."

"Good man, Wiscowicz. Good man."

Buford laughed and bowed, and J. Aubrey allowed himself to be led into his rooms by a pair of Negroes carrying lamps.

When the door was closed behind him he stood patiently while the servants went through lighting lamps and sconces, filling the place with the warm glow of bright light.

Cleotitia, demure, eyes shyly downcast, sat on the floor beside the overstuffed armchair that dominated the sitting room of the sleeping suite. She had her legs curled under her and was quite fetchingly pretty in that pose, at least in J. Aubrey's judgment.

"You, boy," J. Aubrey said harshly to the slave Archimedes. "Light the lamps in my bedroom. And you," he pointed to the other servant, "you may leave now. No, don't say anything. I don't need you sneaking around. Out. Go on now, out."

The man bowed nervously and left in a hurry.

J. Aubrey turned to Ark with a grin and a wink. Cleotitia was looking up now. She came lightly to her feet and ran across the room to throw herself into Ark's embrace.

In spite of himself, J. Aubrey felt a certain amount of moist swelling or fullness in his chest. Probably catching a cold, dammit. He cleared his throat.

"Yes, well, um, don't wake me too early, all right?"

Neither Ark nor Cleotitia was paying much attention to him at the moment.

"Good night," he said. And withdrew silently into the privacy of the bedroom, leaving the newlyweds—courtesy of a ceremony he himself had performed not a dozen hours earlier—to their honeymoon night in Edna Mae Wiscowicz's own impeccably decorated chamber.

FORTY-THREE

"I SAY, Wiscowicz. Is there word from that fool of an army captain yet?"

"No, Your Excellency. Nothing."

J. Aubrey snarled aloud and stomped away to stare out the window. A week had passed since he ordered the Wiscowiczes to send a message to Dinwittie demanding the return of J. Aubrey's luggage. Demanding, that is, the earl's luggage. Which, as it happened, did not in fact exist. During that week the Earl of Whitford had patiently cooperated with Buford and Edna Mae, agreeing to be conspicuously on display as their guest and, by implied association, as their mentor at more soirees, at picnics, even at another of the outdoor events referred to hereabouts as barbecues. One function or another had been scheduled on nearly a daily basis but not once had he demurred or pleaded fatigue. As a houseguest the Earl of Whitford was a jewel among men. But now his good humor seemed to be wearing thin. Seemed, in fact, to have worn completely away.

"Is something wrong, Your Excellency?"

"Wrong? O' course there's something wrong, man. Those fools haven't found my luggage, that's what's wrong."

"I didn't know. . . ."

"Didn't know they haven't found it? How could you not know? D'you see it here? Well, do you? Do you?" The earl paced and wrung his hands. His face turned a dark, plum-like hue of red as he beetled from window to fireplace and back again, wringing his hands all the while and grumbling under his breath.

"No, of course not, Your Excellency," Buford stammered. "But the army hasn't . . . that is to say, your retainers—"

"Damn the army. Damn my servants too. Just find my baggage."

Wiscowicz seemed quite taken aback. "Your servants . . . that is, I thought that you . . . that they—"

"Never mind them, I tell you. Find . . . my . . . *luggage!*" He screamed out the last word into Wiscowicz's startled face, spun round on his heels and went streaking from the room at a most unseemly clip.

Still in this state of intense agitation, the Earl of Whitford took the staircase nearly at a run and swept into the privacy of his suite of rooms with a crash of stamping feet and the clatter of banging doors.

Once he was within, however, he stopped and sent a perfectly beatific smile in the direction of Cleotitia and Archimedes, whom he had interrupted in the midst of a marital embrace. Not bothering to acknowledge the blissful couple's embarrassment—if indeed he noticed it—J. Aubrey winked in their direction and chuckled aloud. The storm clouds had fled from his countenance as if by a miracle and once again he was smiling and sparkling with genial good will.

"Oops," he muttered, finally recognizing the situation that existed upon the sitting room divan. "Sorry." And, whistling a light tune, he made an unhurried departure into the small boudoir where with an air of contentment he laid out a deck of cards and began practicing certain of the mechanic's arts. There no longer existed any trace of the apoplectic dudgeon that had been so vociferously, and unexpectedly, obvious in the Wiscowicz library below.

FORTY-FOUR

HE BOWED. "Miss Cowpen."

She curtsied. "Your Highness." The form of address was inappropriate. He did not correct her. His position was delicate enough without introducing extraneous annoyances. Behind Alexandra half a dozen feet or so stood her father, the man's features reflecting pride and worry and probably half a dozen other emotions that the childless could never hope to decipher. J. Aubrey, that is to say the Earl of Whitford, had come to call at the Cowpen home. If the mountain refuses to come to Muhammad . . .

Not that he was dropping in unannounced. Hardly that. Intercessory pleas had been made. Notes passed. Permissions obtained. Not an invitation exactly but a permission nonetheless. Now the Earl of Whitford, with carriage and borrowed retainers and a vast hamper of foodstuffs, was delighting in the appearance of Alexandra. And unobtrusively assessing Alexander as well.

Cowpen père was not so handsome as Cowpen fille. The daughter's marvelous good looks obviously came from the mother, of whom there was neither presence nor mention.

J. Aubrey made a leg before the lass—it was a convention he was able to carry off with considerable charm and grace if he did say so himself—and carefully refrained from making contact with her gloved fingertips. That, he well knew, was the sort of thing a careful father would note. And of which even a careful father would approve. Then, quickly, he left the girl behind and approached the father. This time his bow of greeting was no more than a stiffly presented nod. After all, one mustn't allow the commoners to forget their place. "Cowpen."

"Yes, Your, um . . ."

"Excellency," J. Aubrey suggested.

Alexander Cowpen looked like he had a fish bone lodged crossways in his throat but he managed to get it out. "Your Excellency."

J. Aubrey sniffed haughtily. Then winked. "A more pleasant meeting than our last, eh?"

Cowpen snorted. Blinked. Became a bit flushed and flustered. "I was hoping you'd forgotten that," he admitted.

"And so I have," J. Aubrey assured him.

"Yes, well, um . . ."

"Have no fear, Cowpen. I shall have your charming daughter home before vespers." J. Aubrey wasn't entirely sure when vespers was, but he had the distinct impression that it was an evening event of some sort. Probably Cowpen wouldn't know either. And anyway it sounded good. "Alexandra?" He offered his arm.

"Yes, Your Excellency," she demurely whispered. She laid a hand lightly on his forearm.

"Cowpen." J. Aubrey touched the brim of his freshly brushed hat.

"Your, um, Excellency."

The handsome couple moved elegantly down the three steps from porch to ground level—the Cowpen house was not a tenth so grand as the Wiscowicz mansion—and on to the carriage where Archimedes served as driver and Cleotitia as maid-in-waiting. That arrangement had seemed an eminently sensible one to J. Aubrey even if it had quite thoroughly confounded Buford Wiscowicz when the earl proposed it. But then poor Buford suffered a number of misapprehensions concerning the earl's supposed relationship with the servant girl Cleotitia and the suddenly, and seriously, devoted manservant Archimedes.

For that matter, Alexander Cowpen likely held to no small

few erroneous assumptions as well, insofar as he believed Archimedes and Cleotitia would function as chaperones of a sort. They, J. Aubrey knew, would seek their own privacy immediately a streamside glade was reached and the comestibles laid out.

And once J. Aubrey was alone with this tender morsel Alexandra . . . such opportunity was an exploration he was ever eager to undertake.

"Now, my dear," he said solicitously, "tell me about yourself." He smiled. "I want to know everything."

FORTY-FIVE

THE EARL OF WHITFORD reached for the glass with a trembling hand. He took the whiskey gratefully and tossed it back in a single draught. "Another. Quickly, man." The Negro poured. The earl drank it quickly down also, then accepted a third and sank back into the lush depths of the overstuffed armchair that dominated the Wiscowicz parlor.

"Didn't you have yourself a nice picnic t'day, Your Excellency?" Edna Mae asked.

"No, that was pleasant. Most enjoyable, in fact. It is just that I was hoping . . ." He let the remainder die unspoken, shaking his head sadly at its passage.

For the past two weeks now the earl's days had been more or less alternating between public functions meant to glorify the Wiscowiczes and private ones meant to entertain the visiting nobleman. That is to say, on one day he might preside over a soiree conceived by Edna Mae, on the next he would call upon Miss Alexandra Cowpen and escort her on a drive under the watchful chaperonage of his borrowed servants.

The time had, in fact, passed delightfully so far as J. Aubrey was concerned. He quite wished he could continue this pattern indefinitely.

But a man shouldn't grow too greedy. Nor trust to Dame Fortune too implicitly. Every gamesman knows there must be limits to all things, good or bad. And that the dictates of timing must never be ignored merely for the sake of a good time.

Alexandra, he feared, would soon have to get along with-

out the companionship of her very own oogledy—her term
—earl.

"Isn't there something we could do, Your Excellency?"
Buford offered. "Anything a'tall. Reckon you know that.
Least I hope you do. Me and Edna Mae would do any ol'
thing for you."

"You and your sister have become quite dear to me,
Buford. If I may unbend so far as to say so."

Edna Mae blushed. So did Buford, a little. They were not
accustomed to the grand Earl of Whitford being so informal
with them.

"Your Excellency . . ." Buford hadn't the words to express his emotion. His mouth opened and closed sound-
lessly. After several attempts to speak he simply shook his
head.

"What Bufe is tryin' to say, Your Excellency, is that
we . . . that is . . . anything, anything a'tall. . . ."

"I understand what you are telling me, dear lady, dear
friends. And so you have become. You really are my friends,
aren't you?"

"Just as deep an' true as ever you'll allow us t' be, Your
Excellency," Buford swore.

J. Aubrey—the earl, that is—sighed and looked deep into
his glass, as if somewhere within the amber liquor there
might be an answer. Then, so softly his listeners had to bend
forward to hear, he spoke again.

"Time," he said. "Time is such a cruel master. And so too
is obligation. Promise. Honor. They all are relentless, dear
friends." And then, as if that had explained everything, he
set the glass aside, leaned his head back against the hand-
tatted antimacassar and closed his eyes.

J. Aubrey didn't have to see to know that Buford and
Edna Mae were exchanging glances of deep concern. He
allowed them ample time for their puzzlement to grow before once more he softly, haltingly spoke.

"Even those of high title must earn their keep, you know.

Those of us who aren't privileged to draw remittances. Of course I shall get on regardless. It's only one opportunity lost, eh? Regrettable that the others must suffer, though. Should've known, what? Shouldn't have allowed others to invest. Should've known better. Now, poof, all over and done with. Investment off God knows where, prob'ly decorating some red savage's greasy braids. Damned Injians wouldn't even know what they have, eh? Too late now t' get replacement back from dear England. Not the sort o' thing even I could ask the Embassy to take on. Had our chance, though. Sound plan is what I say. Opportunity. Wonderful opportunity." He sighed. "Oh, well. Swallow the losses and go on. Only thing t' do, y'see. Stiff upper lip an' all of that, what?" Without opening his eyes he groped back and forth on the surface of the chairside table until he found the whiskey glass and raised it to his lips, drank sparingly of the liquor and cradled the glass beneath his chin. "Nothing else t' do," he whispered. "Damned shame, that's what it is."

"Your Excellency. Please. Me an' Bufe, we don' know what you're sayin'. But if there's anything we can do. . . ."

"Secrets," the earl mumbled. "Promised my partners, don't you see. Can't disclose their interest in the venture. Can't be known that they're allied with me in business. Political reasons, don't you see. Can't let their names be bandied about. An' without replacement of the lost capital can't put the deal across. Damned shame is what it is. Profit enough to set us all up for life." He snorted. "Damned shame." He drank off the last of the whiskey. Sank lower into his chair. In a few moments more he began to snore very lightly. The empty glass dropped from his fingers and rolled into his lap.

Buford and Edna Mae exchanged more looks, these perhaps even more puzzled than the earlier ones had been, before finally they rose from their chairs and tiptoed silently out of the room.

FORTY-SIX

THE DAY'S PLAN called for a dinner party attended by thirty or so intimate friends. More accurately, a dinner party attended by people who Buford and Edna Mae hoped would become intimate friends.

After so many such functions J. Aubrey had learned to recognize the targets of such affairs. There was always a cadre of regulars in attendance, a group of residents whose thoughts and politics melded with those of the Wiscowiczes. That group included the Dockerys, the Armbristers, the Cordells and a few others. Then there was a secondary group who were already swayed and could be counted upon to support Buford when things came to a head—whenever that event might occur and whatever it proved to be; J. Aubrey hadn't the slightest inkling what the future held for Kansas nor just how Buford and his supporters intended to sway those decisions—and who now were being rewarded. And then finally there was the much smaller number of guests, never more than half a dozen at any one event, who were the objects of interest for that particular affair.

Those people would be given the privilege of access to the titled visitor from afar. They would be personally introduced to the Earl of Whitford and, one way or another, placed close to him during the course of the event. More to the point, these individuals would be fawned upon and flattered by Buford and by Edna Mae. And each of them would be assigned close attendance by one of the cadre of solid regulars like the Dockerys.

On more than one occasion J. Aubrey noticed Sue Dockery's flirtations with a male target. And on more than one occasion he noticed that both Mrs. Dockery and her target of the evening would briefly disappear, soon to return in states of seeming contentment and great relaxation. J. Aubrey was almost tempted to see what it was he was missing. But only almost.

The evening following the earl's whiskey-induced unbending—which no one mentioned the entire day long—J. Aubrey went through all the motions expected of him, plus he made it a point to mention several times over how very much he personally appreciated the Wiscowiczes and all their kindness. By the conclusion of the dinner both Buford and Edna Mae were fair beaming with pride. And it was apparent that the targets of the evening were thoroughly impressed with the charm and the leadership capabilities of Buford Wiscowicz, Esq. J. Aubrey thought it particularly nice to see his host and hostess so happy.

"Join me for a nightcap, Your Excellency?" Buford suggested after the last of the guests departed.

"Thank you, yes." Out of the corner of his eye J. Aubrey caught sight of the nod Buford gave to his sister.

"You boys have yourselves a nice time, hear? I got to go up to bed," Edna Mae said in response to her cue. "It's been a real long day."

The Earl of Whitford, ever the gallant gentleman, bowed low over her hand and loudly kissed the air a half inch or so from her flesh. Edna Mae simpered and scampered—well, as much as it was possible for a woman of her bulk to scamper—off to the stairs.

"Your Excellency?" Buford pointed the now entirely familiar way to the library, eschewing use of the parlor since dear Edna Mae would not be able to join them.

"Thengkew." J. Aubrey had heard an Englishman say it that way once. It had sounded silly then, less so now. In fact, he suspected he would rather miss a great many aspects of this particular role when he had to leave it behind.

As he very soon, and very completely, would be forced to do.

He allowed himself to be escorted into the library where a cheery fire had been laid against the fall chill and where a thin Negro named Dante waited with a serving tray, lap robes and whatever other comforts the gentlemen might require.

"Whiskey, champagne, brandy?"

"Brandy, I think. But only a drop."

Buford nodded and motioned for Dante to comply, which the servant quickly did.

"Thengkew." The earl's response was, quite properly, addressed to the master, not the man.

"My pleasure," Buford said.

"Buford . . . may I call you Buford?"

"Oh yes, Your Excellency. An honor." And indeed he looked as pleased as if he'd just been knighted.

J. Aubrey was careful to suggest no such familiarity between Buford and himself, however. He sniffed. Very lightly. And said, "I may have made certain, um, statements, Buford. Last night. Regrettable. I was out of line. I hope you will accept my apologies. And, mm, forget anything you may have heard as well."

"Your Excellency. Please! There's no reason for you t' apologize. No, sir, not a one. Why, I only wisht there was something me and Edna Mae could do to help out. Fact is, Your Excellency, that's why I asked Edna Mae to leave you an' me be this evening. I was wanting to have a word with you in private. Just you an' me alone here." It seemed honestly not to occur to the man that Dante and his tray were hovering only a few paces away. Dante could hear every word spoken without any effort, in truth would not be able to avoid overhearing even if he wished. But then Dante was less than human, wasn't he. J. Aubrey still found such distinctions to be interesting.

The Earl of Whitford's grunt was noncommittal. He smelled of the brandy he held but did not taste it yet.

"The thing is," Buford said, taking J. Aubrey's silence for assent, "me and Edna Mae couldn't help but hear what you was saying. Not that we understood much of it, mind. But enough to kinda get the gist o' things. Way we understand it, Your Excellency, you an' some friends in England got you something going. Some real good investment deal. And o' course that's none o' our business. Me and Edna Mae would be the first to own up to that. What you got going ain't any of our nevermind. But from what you was sayin' last night, the capital you an' your English pals put up was in the baggage you was carrying when you got took by them Indians. Is that right, Your Excellency? I don't mean t' pry. I want you t' understand that. But I got a reason for asking."

The Earl of Whitford scowled and peered into the fire for long moments before he answered. "My problem, Buford, is that I am constrained by questions of privacy. My partners—"

"Lordy, Your Excellency," Buford was quick to inject. "Me and Edna Mae don't wanta know who your partners are. No reason why we should. Comes t' that, ha ha, you could tell us their names an' we still wouldn't know. Only Englishman either of us has ever met is you yourself, Your Excellency. Wouldn't a single one o' them names mean nothing to us."

"Mm, I can see that that would be so," the earl agreed.

"The thing is, Your Excellency, you got you something going an' now through no fault o' your own you've lost, just till you can get hold o' your pals back in England, but it looks like you've lost your capital an' stand t' lose your opportunity too. If we understood what we thought we did last night, that is. Not that it's any o' our business." The man was sitting on the forward edge of his chair, practically aquiver with the plan he intended to propose to the great man; a plan which he would be certain the earl could not possibly anticipate. Buford looked as eager as a puppy wagging its tail outside a butcher shop's back door. In either case, J. Aubrey thought, whether for the factual Buford or the figurative pup, the scent from within must have been nigh unendurable.

"I would say," the earl intoned after judicious consideration, "that you correctly apprehend the essential facts of my situation. Not that I intended to burden you and your dear sister with my personal difficulties, of course. Please accept my apologies for allowing it to happen."

"There's no need for that, Your Excellency. Honest there isn't. But like I told you, me and Edna Mae talked this over between us. What we'd like t' do—and believe me, you won't ever have to say a word to us about your partners back home, won't even have to tell them about us if you don't want—but what we'd like to do, Your Excellency, is for us to front your investment capital—no, don't say no till you've heard me out, please—and then you can either leave us in as silent partners or just pay us back whenever it's convenient, however you'd like t' do it, Your Excellency."

"Buford!" the Earl of Whitford gasped. "I . . . I am stunned, sir. Positively stunned."

J. Aubrey hoped that he managed to so appear. Never mind that it had taken him weeks to arrange things so that Buford and his dear sister would conceive this entirely, um, unexpected idea.

He was able, somehow, to keep from laughing.

"You don't have t' say anything right now," Buford hastened to add. "In fact, please don't. Sleep on it, Your Excellency. Think about it tonight. We'll talk some more tomorra."

The Earl of Whitford sighed, frowned, nodded. "I believe that may be wise, Buford. We shall talk again tomorrow, dear friend."

Buford beamed and signaled for Dante to refill their glasses, although the earl had not yet partaken.

"If you would excuse me, Buford," J. Aubrey said, rising,

"I suspect I shall be up quite late tonight. I've much to think about, don't I?"

Buford beamed all the brighter and bobbed his head. If the man became any more eager, J. Aubrey thought, he would begin to drool. That was a sight one would prefer to forgo. "Good night, friend Buford."

"G'night, Your Excellency."

J. Aubrey was smiling as he mounted the stairs toward his suite.

FORTY-SEVEN

"DEAR FRIENDS," the earl said with a sigh. "My dear, dear friends." The three of them, J. Aubrey and Buford and Edna Mae, were dining en famille in the informal breakfast room —the servants, of course, did not count. The Earl of Whitford had spent the afternoon driving out with Miss Alexandra Cowpen and several of her lady friends—a most enjoyable afternoon it had been, too—but returned earlier than was his norm on such occasions. If Buford Wiscowicz wanted to believe that J. Aubrey hurried back on his account, well, that would only be accurate. Not that the precise nature of that eagerness would be as Buford believed. But the earl's anticipation was nonetheless genuine. "I have been thinking about what we, mm, discussed last night, Buford."

Buford coughed into his napkin and replaced it in his lap, his hand remaining out of sight beneath the edge of the table. From the angle of his arm, though, J. Aubrey could see with considerable amusement what the fellow was doing. He was squeezing his sister's hand. As if in triumph. J. Aubrey smiled.

"Your offer is generous in the extreme," the Earl of Whitford said. "But I could not possibly ask you to—what is the quaint saying you colonials use?—buy a pig in a poke like that." J. Aubrey shook his head and reached for his cup. Tea, of course. Inevitably tea out of respect for his supposed wishes. That was one thing he would be almighty glad to see changed when he left here. It would be damnably nice to be able to have coffee again for a change.

Buford's face drained of all color. Edna Mae looked like she might break into tears.

The Earl of Whitford set his teacup down again. "It wouldn't be fair to you, Buford."

"But . . . but . . ."

"Not unless you are aware of what we propose and fully approve of it. I've thought this over, as you asked me to do. That is the conclusion I reached. I could not possibly accept your assistance unless you fully concurred with the plan and wished to become a true partner in the venture."

My, how the expressions on the other side of the table did change. Where there had been despair, hope blossomed anew. Joy unbounded filled their eyes. Buford's hand moved slightly beneath the edge of the table as he squeezed over and over again. Edna Mae's eyelashes fluttered so rapidly J. Aubrey feared she might create a whirlwind.

"Really, Your Excellency, anything you wish—"

"No, Buford, I insist. Truly I do. I shall not accept your generous offer unless you fully approve. But, frankly," he leaned forward and glanced about the room with a conspiratorial air, then lowered his voice, "but frankly, friends, I think I know where your sympathies lie."

Buford looked puzzled.

J. Aubrey was gilding the lily again. This line wasn't really necessary. He knew that. Poor old Buford would hand over anything the earl wanted, at once and without a whimper. But, dammit, J. Aubrey'd come up with a plan calculated to appeal to a number of different impulses. There wasn't any reason not to use it all. So he might as well go the last mile and make the Wiscowiczes all that much more anxious to part with the war chest they'd been given by all those other slaveholding Southerners.

"You already know, Buford, that England's sympathies have always lain with the planters of your southern states."

Buford nodded. "Naturally, Your Excellency. Our cotton and your mills. We need each other."

"Precisely," J. Aubrey agreed. "But the union is expanding. There is sentiment in some quarters in the north of your country to strangle the south. For reasons which I shan't mention, my own country having abolished certain, um, ancient institutions, and my own relatives having been prominent in that unwise decision," he cut his eyes in the direction of the servants who were standing patiently nearby, "but upon which you and I concur, mm?"

"Yes, I do understand," Buford said sagely. "You mentioned political considerations at home. This would—"

J. Aubrey coughed loudly and laid a cautionary finger to his lips. "There are things best left unspoken, mm?"

"Yes. Sorry." Buford didn't look the least bit sorry. If anything he looked rather like the cat whose mouth is ringed with tiny yellow feathers . . . but which denies knowledge of the canary cage door having been left ajar.

"Suffice it to say, friend Buford, that we share certain cherished beliefs. And that some of us in dear auld England are supportive of our fellow thinkers on this side of the waters, what?"

"Ah! I see," Buford exclaimed. Although he didn't.

"We are not altogether altruistic, however," the Earl of Whitford admitted. "We find nothing wrong with being supportive of our friends and, well, lining our own pockets at the same time."

"Yes?"

"Our proposal, Buford, is to create a commercial link between your south and the wealth of the Santa Fe trade."

Buford looked blank. Edna Mae glanced at her brother. "Bufe?"

"Shush."

The Earl of Whitford endowed them with an indulgent smile. "I see you fail to take my point."

"Reckon we ought to. But—"

"Factions in the north of your country would limit the

wealth and the power of the south if they were able to do so, is that not true?"

"They sure would."

"But if the south held control not only of the present trade with England but control as well of all the traffic now flowing over your Santa Fe Trail?"

"The National Road, Your Excellency, runs from Missoura. An' it's a long way from set which way Missoura an' someday Kansas are gonna go when it comes to . . . you know." And he too sent a significant glance in the direction of the Negroes.

The Earl of Whitford continued to smile.

"Might a railroad linking New Orleans and Santa Fe by way of Vicksburg and West Port make a difference, Buford?"

Buford gasped. Edna Mae looked like she might faint dead away. "A railroad?"

"Between myself and my friends," the Earl of Whitford said without bluster, "we can generate whatever capital is required to realize just such a venture. And it is our belief, Buford, that however much the construction costs, the returns over a period of time, even a brief period, will more than justify the initial expenditures."

"But that could mean . . . why, a railroad all the way from New Orleans . . . that'd join the whole of the west to Looziana an' Miss'sippi an' the rest."

"That is our belief, Buford. That is our belief in a nutshell."

"But you didn't come along with money enough for nothing like that, Your Excellency. I mean . . . not carrying it in your baggage, you didn't."

The earl laughed. "Hardly that, dear Buford. No, what is needed now is a commitment of right-of-way. Can't lay rail without a road, you know. I came here acting on my own behalf and that of my partners to secure certain commitments of land holdings. We already hold options on everything we need between New Orleans and Vicksburg. It was

my next task to secure the same in your Missouri. Which is
what I intended before the diversion forced upon me by the
aboriginals. The problem is that the option must be secured
from a man—I'll not mention his name, but you would recognize it instantly—who must not be known to be in sympathy with us. Very hush-hush, you see. And if we don't
have the deal formalized before the tenth day of November
we shall miss our chance. This man—I wish I could tell you
his name—will be leaving on a journey then. We must strike
now or not at all. So you, um, see my dilemma, don't you?"

"Yes. Course I do. Oh, Lordy, yes," Buford moaned. J.
Aubrey thought sure the fellow was going to drool this time.

"Even so, Buford, I wouldn't think of allowing you to
participate unless you approve of our plan. And unless you
would want to consider accepting a small position in the
stock holdings as soon as the railroad is officially incorpo-
rated in your country. We have a limited partnership of reg-
ister in England, of course. But we dare not incorporate here
until we are willing for our plan to become publicly known,
don't you see." J. Aubrey paused, then snapped his fingers.
"Why didn't I think of this before, Buford? We'll be needing
an American to take out the papers of incorporation anyway. It's a figurehead position, no real responsibility involved, but it's necessary under your laws. Which I'm sure
you already know." If Buford knew any such then it would
come as something of a shock to J. Aubrey; but that was
neither here nor there at the moment. "On the positive side,
old friend, the sinecure does carry with it a two percent
stock position. No telling what that could amount to over
time. I myself expect to become revoltingly wealthy on a
twenty percent stake in the company, eh?" He grinned.

"Good Lord," Buford moaned.

"Oh dear," Edna Mae rasped.

"How . . . how much did you . . . ?"

"The gentleman in Missouri has agreed to grant us the
option we require upon payment of the sum of . . . ," this

was a point over which J. Aubrey had agonized for some weeks now, ". . . twenty-two thousand five hundred." The odd number, J. Aubrey knew, should have the effect of making the amount seem more *official.* So to speak.

This time Buford's reaction was a groan, not a moan. "That much," he grieved aloud.

"I say. I've embarrassed you. I never meant to do that, dear friend. Please forget I ever said anything. Forget it all. Why, I should rather lose a thousand fortunes than cause distress to such wonderful friends as you and Edna Mae. Please forgive me." Quite completely overcome with remorse, the Earl of Whitford jumped up from the table and hurried out of the breakfast room.

He hurried not toward his own suite but outside and in the direction of the barn, where faithful Archimedes by now should be waiting with the carriage. Alexandra had promised to meet him upon moonrise.

Even his anticipation of that event, however, could not keep J. Aubrey from wondering if he'd overestimated the situation here. Twenty-two thousand five hundred dollars was approximately half the wealth of the hemisphere so far as J. Aubrey was concerned. It was so much that he'd had reservations about thinking it, much less naming it to that greedy southern patriot Buford.

But, dammit, it was the figure he came up with when he evaluated the probable worth of the Wiscowicz holdings in land and slaves. And that was without taking into account any cash resources that might be available.

If it proved to be too much, if Buford and Edna Mae balked at giving away the influence money given to them by their southern backers, well, J. Aubrey would think about that if or when the time came. This was his one chance to make history, after all. He was *not* going to do less than lean full out to reach the big brass ring. And if he failed, dammit, then so be it. It wouldn't be for lack of trying.

J. Aubrey Whitford squared his shoulders manfully. Cleared his throat. Shot his cuffs. Smoothed the lapel of his cutaway. "Ready when you are, Ark."

"Yes, suh," Archimedes said and with a wink sent the Wiscowicz carriage rocking into motion.

FORTY-EIGHT

"MM," HE WHISPERED, his breath warm and teasing in her ear.

Alexandra sighed.

"My dear," he said, the sound of it partially muffled because of his lips being nested within the hollow at the base of her throat.

Alexandra wriggled.

"I've a favor to ask of you," he purred against the pale, slim column of her neck.

Alexandra giggled.

"I want to talk with your father," he said.

Alexandra yelped and came bolt upright on the seat of the landau.

FORTY-NINE

BUFORD hooked a forefinger beneath the constricting ring of his shirt collar and tugged the offending material away from the rapidly fluttering pulse in his slightly wattled throat. The man was pale and pasty this morning, and his hands visibly shook. Buford and his unlovely sister were ardent trenchermen—trencherpersons?—and normally could be counted upon to empty a full platter of eggs and ham apiece. This morning only the Earl of Whitford displayed much of an appetite for the array of victuals spread before them in the breakfast room.

J. Aubrey helped himself to a biscuit so light it required a dollop of gravy on top lest it float away from the plate. Baking soda biscuits made in the fashion of the south, he had determined, were a cultural achievement of great and lasting value. He decided to take two. Certainly there was no competition for them being offered by either Buford or Edna Mae, neither of whom looked like he, or she, had slept particularly well. "Wonderful. Simply wonderful," he enthused. "Would you pass the strawberry preserves, please? Thengkew."

"Uh, mm, ahem."

"Yes, Buford?"

"About, um, what you told us last night."

"I do hope you accept my apology. It was thoughtless of me. Forget I said anything. Is that honey-butter over there? Yes, in that crock. Yes. May I have it, please? Wonderful." He reached for another biscuit.

"Your Excellency!" The words came out in a quavering,

tremulous plea. Piercingly loud, startlingly abrupt. The intensity of his voice seemed to surprise even Buford.

"Yes, old friend?"

"We'll do it." Breathless. Rushing to get the words out lest he realize what he was about and come to his senses before he could say it. Frightened of the enormity of this step, that was what his difficulty of the moment truly was. J. Aubrey understood that even if Buford might not.

"Pardon?"

"I said . . . ," deep, gulping breath but no pause for thought, "I said we'll do it. That is, Edna Mae and me, we talked it over last night. Most the whole night long if you want the truth. I mean . . . that's an awful lot of money, Your Excellency. Not for you, o' course. But for any normal folks it's a fortune. But we can swing it. We're sure we can. It'll just take a little time. Not too long. We'll have you fixed up an' on your way in plenty o' time to make that appointment with the fella in Missoura. We'll do it. For sure." Once he'd begun speaking, once the commitment was made, the words came easier to Buford and so did his breathing. In fact, as he spoke he became increasingly calm. Even his complexion improved, the color coming back into his cheeks and the tremors dissipating from his hands. By the time he was done he was able to give the Earl of Whitford a confident smile. And why should he not? Were not the two of them now partners in a common venture, Buford Wiscowicz of old Alabam' and Aubrey, Earl of Whitford, side by side and arm in arm? Of course they were.

"Only if you really want to," J. Aubrey said in a casually offhand tone of voice. "Just don't strap yourself." And he spooned a mound of ruby-colored strawberry preserves onto a biscuit half that was still warm from the oven. Wonderful stuff, really.

Across the table Buford and Edna Mae were clinging tight to one another's hands. The Earl of Whitford affected not to notice.

FIFTY

THREE DAYS, J. Aubrey thought when he saw Buford's surrey coming home at a spanking clip. Three days was all it had taken. Not bad. Not bad at all. He smiled softly to himself and went over to the sideboard to help himself to a brandy—which he most definitely felt he deserved—waving Jason away when the servant hurried toward him from across the room.

"To your good health," J. Aubrey said, lifting his glass to Jason in a mock toast and winking at the man. Jason merely sent back a fearful look and made a hasty departure from the presence of this crazy white man.

Crazy enough, J. Aubrey thought happily. But, oh, he was going to miss the old earl.

Jason being absent now, J. Aubrey found a mirror and toasted himself before he swallowed off the last of the tot. He smacked his lips loudly. And went into the hallway to greet the returning champion.

"I can hardly believe my own good fortune," Buford enthused to an admiring audience that consisted of his sister Miss Edna Mae Wiscowicz, late of Alabama, and his dear friend and business partner, the Earl of Whitford. "I'd expected to have to wait several weeks at the very least before the mortgage money could be obtained. But just recently, Harlan told me, there were investors inquiring for mortgage opportunity here. Just when we needed them. Isn't that a most remarkable coincidence?"

"Remarkable," Edna Mae agreed aloud.

Remarkable, J. Aubrey silently smirked. Aloud, though, he

said, "I wish you hadn't mortgaged your property here, Buford. You know I advised against that."

"We know you did, Your Excellency, and we appreciate your concern for us. But after all, ha ha, in whose hands could anything be safer than yours? Besides, this is no expenditure. It's an investment. Good as gold, ha ha. Better, even. Why, with a percentage of ownership in the railroad, Edna Mae and I, and all of our, um, backers—have I told you about our friends back home, Your Excellency? I must; I know you will appreciate them and what they, we all, are trying to do here—in any event, with that percentage of ownership we can count on profits for years and years to come. Our work here, elsewhere too, will proceed beyond our wildest hopes. And it is all arranged now. Everything complete. All the papers have been signed. Why, it was even possible to get currency for you instead of specie." He pointed to a thick, oilcloth-bound packet atop his desk. J. Aubrey had wondered how large a lump twenty-two thousand five hundred dollars in cash would make. Now he knew. "Isn't that remarkable? And in this country where specie is so much more common than paper currency, too. I tell you, all these wonderful coincidences, everything falling together so nicely, it just goes to show, Your Excellency, that this whole thing was fated to turn out as it has. Positively fated, I tell you."

"Positively," Edna Mae agreed aloud.

J. Aubrey merely smiled and bobbed his head happily.

"You will stay here until it's time for you to go meet the gentleman from Missoura, won't you?"

"Certainly. And I'll return here afterward if I may. Report on our venture and all that. Meanwhile, Buford, whyn't you put that package out of sight in that drawer. I won't be needing it until I'm ready to leave, you know. I suggest you tend to it until then, what?" The Earl of Whitford smiled. So, inwardly, and for different reasons, did J. Aubrey.

"You are always an honored guest in this house, Your Excellency."

"Thengkew, dear friend." The earl raised his glass in a toast. J. Aubrey smiled. And smiled. And smiled.

FIFTY-ONE

THE EARL OF WHITFORD dabbed at his lips with a crisp, freshly starched and ironed linen napkin. "If you would excuse me . . . ?"

"Oh, but, Your Excellency," Edna Mae whined, "I told the cook to make us somethin' special for dessert t'night. You can't leave yet."

"Ah, dear lady, you know how I adore your desserts," he said smoothly, thinking to himself that truly tonight the lady would receive her just desserts. And so would her brother. "But I made promises to a certain young lady. Would that I had known we should have cause to celebrate, eh? But I didn't. And a promise made is a promise that must be kept. I know you will understand."

Edna Mae pouted but Buford, all bright smiles and vibrant energy since his triumphal homecoming earlier in the afternoon, made her hush. Buford very likely wanted some privacy anyway in which he could bask in the warmth of Edna Mae's admiration and not have to share the glory, not even with his dear chum and business partner the Earl of Whitford.

"May I have the use of the carriage and servants for the evening, Buford?"

Buford appeared stricken, aghast. "How could you ask a question like that? You know, Your Excellency, that everything we have is yours."

"Mm, yes." J. Aubrey smiled. "So it is." His belly fluttered but he managed to contain the laughter. "Good night, Edna Mae." He bent over her hand, the very image of the gallant gentleman. "Friend Buford." He clicked his heels sharply and bowed. "Au revoir."

"Huh?"

"I said good night."

"Oh. Right. G'night, Your Excellency."

The Earl of Whitford made an unhurried departure from the dining room, stopped briefly in the library where Buford's big desk was housed and went upstairs to complete his preparations for the evening.

FIFTY-TWO

J. AUBREY felt a trifle uncomfortable as he paused upon the porch outside the Cowpen residence. He knew what caused his discomfort. And that cause had nothing to do with facing the man who happened to be Alexandra's father. It was simply that he, well, *bulged*.

With so much paper of one kind or another stuffed into this pocket or behind that fastener, why, the lines of his coat were ruined, that was all. Simply ruined no matter how he tugged and tucked. J. Aubrey hated ill-fitting clothes. Fortunately he wouldn't have to put up with them much longer. Just as soon as he reached a suitable haven . . .

He pushed and pulled and rearranged once more the lump of folded papers that filled his inside left-hand coat pocket. That particular wad represented papers of manumission for the former slaves known as Archimedes and Cleotitia Whitford—well, he was entitled to some small conceit here, wasn't he? and it wasn't as though they had surnames of their own—including certified statements proving that the manumissions were duly and properly recorded at the courthouse in Whitelaw, Mississippi. Not that J. Aubrey had any idea if such a town existed. But then no one else was apt to be certain that Whitelaw, Mississippi—the invented name amused him and could be of no harm—did *not* exist. J. Aubrey's sure hands and gold pen nibs had created the documents—he'd had to do something with all his free time of late, hadn't he? He was sure none of those papers would be questioned.

In the interior right-hand coat pocket he had another

lump that represented a sampling of bearer bonds, letters of credit and the like.

Scattered here and there about his person there was also an assortment of cartes de visite, letters addressed to him at various different addresses and referring to him as the practitioner of this profession or of that pursuit. A gentleman never knew what might prove useful in the future. It never hurt to be prepared for a number of differing eventualities.

And there had been, after all, a great deal of free time available.

As for the other lumps and bulges, well, they were the most satisfying of all. And the genuine article too. Not even J. Aubrey's fine hand could create engraving of such delicate artistry or paper of that peculiar grade and content. The forging of paper currency was something he had too much pride even to attempt. J. Aubrey Whitford was not a man who sought failure.

What he did seek at the moment was a word with Alexander Cowpen. He cleared his throat, made one last attempt to arrange his clothing satisfactorily and, deeming that a hopeless cause, knocked upon the Cowpen door.

FIFTY-THREE

"NO, THANK YOU, Mr. Cowpen, I believe I've had enough for tonight. One has to maintain one's wits, eh?" the Earl of Whitford said in his final moments under that nom de guerre. His words were certainly true enough, however false his identity. "I'll not intrude upon your evening, sir. Pity I've missed finding your lovely daughter at home though, mm? You must express my regrets at having missed her." Never mind that he himself had only hours earlier sent certain notes to Alexandra's dearest friends suggesting how touched the young lady would be were she the recipient of a surprise party. He was pleased now to think that at this moment Alexandra and her friends should be enjoying innocent pleasures round the piano in Martha Jane Reeves's parlor.

"Tell me once more, Your Excellency . . . ?"

The Earl of Whitford graced the man with an indulgent smile. "As I already explained, man, the knowledge I gained in that household convinces me. Your people will soon be in possession of all the Southerners' property. Wiscowicz shan't be able to make the mortgage payment. If the document were written as a demand note as I suggested, sir, you can foreclose at your leisure and dispose of the assets to your advantage. Mind, though. You made a sacred promise to me. I expect you to discharge it in the fullest extent."

"That, Your Excellency, is something we see eye to eye about. Probably the only thing we agree on, I'd say. But on this point we have no quarrel. As soon as my people gain title, sir, we shall manumit every slave owned by Wiscowicz and his crowd. We would do that even in the absence of any promises, sir, I assure you."

The Earl of Whitford grunted. And sniffed. Loudly and with just the slightest hint of disdain. Too bad he was going to have to abandon the sniff just when he'd learned to master it in all its shadings and nuances.

"But are you sure—?"

"Of course I am sure, man. D'you think I would have approached you with the scheme otherwise? No profit in this to me, you know. Simply wishing to do my duty as a gentleman. And I thought you would want to do the same. We English abhor involuntary servitude, y'know. Can't abide the fact that it's so prevalent here in the colonies, what?"

"It hasn't been long since you abolished it yourselves," Cowpen said.

The Earl of Whitford sniffed. It was on this occasion a defensive measure. He hadn't actually been sure that the English disavowed slavery, not until he'd gotten Buford to talking on the subject one evening. And then he certainly hadn't dared inquire about the specifics of their system.

"Great-Aunt Victoria's politics aside, Cowpen, I personally have abhorred the institution for quite as long as I can recall."

"And so you should, Your Excellency. So should we all."

The earl sniffed again, enjoying the use of it while he still could.

"Anyway," the Earl of Whitford said crisply. "Thought I should mention the success of your efforts. Since I happened to be here hoping t' see Miss Cowpen. Please convey my compliments to your charming daughter and express to her my, um, deepest regrets at having missed her."

"I'll do that, Your Excellency."

J. Aubrey started toward the door, stopped once there and turned back into the small vestibule. He smiled. "Oh yes. Almost forgot, what? Might as well leave it now that I'm here. A jotting, you see. Something I thought Miss Cowpen might find amusing." He pulled a sealed envelope from a pocket—the effect of its absence upon the fit of his coat was no doubt salutary—and handed the slim packet over to Cowpen.

"I'll see that she gets this as soon as she returns home," Cowpen promised.

"Thengkew." J. Aubrey smiled and touched the brim of his hat. "Good evening, sir." And he disappeared into the night.

FIFTY-FOUR

My Dearest Alexandra:

It is with the deepest regret that I make this confession to you, my darling girl. It is necessary for me to make my departure, for reasons which soon must become apparent to you and to the community of Cowpen's Lick. I could not bear to leave, dearest, without giving to you both my confession and my explanation.

First permit me to confess that I am not the Earl of Whitford nor even an Englishman, nor is my true name Whitford. Mr. J. Aubrey Whitford is a gentleman I met recently in Texas and whose name I borrowed for this occasion, it being for no particular reason the first to come into my thoughts. It is my hope that my recent activities will not redound to that worthy gentleman's disadvantage.

By way of explanation, darling, my deception was cruel to you but beneficial to certain others, as your father shall be able to explain in greater detail than is necessary here. Suffice it to say that I am proud of the purpose your father and I shared here.

Nor is that the only thing upon which your father and I agree. Both of us, you see, believe you to be the sweetest, the prettiest, the most dear and precious creature in all this soon-to-be territory. That, darling, you must always believe.

As for my failings, dearest, I can only plead guilty with the aforementioned mitigation. I am a base, crass, fallible human. I can be no more than I am, although were it

should be happy to change for your sweet

said (and I do hope, dear one, that you will be
nough to refrain from allowing this missive to fall
hands other than your own so gentle ones), it is my
that you would forgive me to the extent of granting
one last favor.

Please, my precious Alexandra, broadcast throughout
the community the knowledge I have herein given you.
My reason for asking this of you is a belief that Wiscowicz
and his ilk will be more deeply and more permanently
wounded by laughter than by mere financial reversal. It is
for this reason, dearest, that I ask you to assure that all
know he was deceived, gulled, quite happily humiliated
by a pretender who was neither earl nor kindred spirit.
You should, of course, feel free to discuss this with your
father before you act upon my petition.

I wish for you to know, darling Alexandra, that this
matter was the only deception I engaged upon while in
your presence. As for the words we whispered one to
another in our moments of privacy, those were and remain heartfelt and true.

And now, my dear one, I regretfully close this message
and beg your indulgence and your understanding if not
your continued high regard.

With deepest affection always, I am (or in any event
briefly was),
Aubrey, Earl of Whitford

ABOUT THE AUTHOR

FRANK RODERUS is the author of twenty Double D Westerns, including *Leaving Kansas,* which won the Western Writers of America's Spur Award in 1983. He has been a Spur Award finalist six times, and his work has been reprinted in Great Britain, Germany, Italy, Norway, and Finland. He lives in Sarasota, Florida.